my LITTLE PONY
Friendship is Magic
SEASON 10

VOLUME
2

Facebook: **facebook.com/idwpublishing**
Twitter: **@idwpublishing**
YouTube: **youtube.com/idwpublishing**
Instagram: **@idwpublishing**

Cover Artist
Brianna Garcia

Series Editor
Megan Brown

Group Editor
Bobby Curnow

Collection Editors
Alonzo Simon
& Zac Boone

Collection Designer
Jessica Gonzalez

IDW

Licensed By:

Hasbro

ISBN: 978-1-68405-845-7 24 23 22 21 1 2 3 4

Originally published as MY LITTLE PONY: FRIENDSHIP IS MAGIC issues #94–97 and MY LITTLE PONY: FRIENDSHIP IS MAGIC ANNUAL 2021.

Special thanks to Ed Lane, Beth Artale, and Michael Kelly.

Something There That Wasn't Before

WRITTEN BY THOM ZAHLER

ART BY TONI KUUSISTO

The Two Kingdoms of Caninia

WRITTEN BY JEREMY WHITLEY

ART BY BRIANNA GARCIA

Abyssinians

WRITTEN BY JEREMY WHITLEY

ART BY TONY FLEECS

COLORS BY HEATHER BRECKEL

LETTERS BY NEIL UYETAKE

SOMETHING THERE THAT WASN'T BEFORE

CANTERLOT...
STOP IT! STOP! STOP!
THOSE ARE OFF-MODEL!

DO YOU THINK THOSE ICE SCULPTURES CAPTURE THE INEFFABLE GRACE OF THE PRINCESSES?
THIS IS THE FIRST FESTIVAL OF THE TWO SISTERS SINCE THE PRINCESSES RETIRED! WE NEED TO MAKE THIS ONE PERFECT.
TWILIGHT! IT'S GOING TO BE OKAY.
THE FIRST FESTIVAL WAS PERFECT, BUT IT HAD THE PRINCESSES!
THIS IS THE FIRST ONE WITHOUT THEM, AND IT'S GOING TO SET THE TONE FOR THE REST.
IT HAS TO BE PERFECT.
IT WILL BE, TWILIGHT. DON'T WORRY.
REALLY? IT WILL? BECAUSE WHERE IS SHE? SHE SAID SHE'D BE HERE.
FLAP!
HAVE NO FEAR! PINKIE PIE HAS ARRIVED!
WAIT, THAT'S NOT RIGHT. CAN I GO OUT AND COME BACK IN AGAIN? I MESSED UP THE RHYME.
SHIELD HORSE

NO! NOT AT ALL! YOUR ENTRANCE WAS PERFECT.
CAN YOU SAVE OUR CELEBRATION?
ARE YOU KIDDING? IT'LL BE A **SAVE**ABRATION!
NOTES OF PARTY LIFE
HERE'S WHAT I'VE COME UP WITH SO FAR.
HAYBURGERS!
SO, HOW BAD IS IT?
WELL, I CAN'T SAY I WOULD HAVE THOUGHT OF HAVING A GROUP READ-IN. THAT'S... INTERESTING.
OVERALL, IT'S A SOLID START, TWILIGHT.
A SOLID START?! ***A SOLID START?!***
THAT'S WHAT CELESTIA USED TO TELL ME WHEN I WAS NOWHERE NEAR DONE WITH MY HOMEWORK.
THAT'S THE WORST THING YOU COULD HAVE SAID!

WE SHOULD HAVE SOME BALLOON ANIMALS. I REMEMBER **CHEESE SANDWICH** THREW A PARTY WHERE HE DID BALLOON CARICATURES OF PONIES. THAT WENT OVER REALLY, REALLY WELL.
OUR MUSICAL ACTS SEEM GOOD. THOUGH I MIGHT NOT HAVE THE ATONAL APALOOSAN THROAT SINGERS ON THE MAIN STAGE.
THE COLORS ON THE STAGE COULD USE A LITTLE MORE CONTRAST, CHEESE ALWAYS SAYS TO HAVE A UNIFIED ACCENT COLOR.
OR DID HE SAY TO HAVE A SILLY ACCENT? PROBABLY BOTH.
YEAH, WE SHOULD DEFINITELY HAVE GAMING BOOTHS OVER THERE. CHEESE SAYS PIN THE TAIL ON THE DRAGON ALWAYS WORKS. AND A BALLOON POP.
OH, YEAH, WE DEFINITELY NEED T-SHIRTS! I JUST NEED TO REMEMBER THE PRINTER CHEESE USED...
WE'LL HAVE TO FIGURE OUT HOTELS, OF COURSE.
YOU KNOW, THIS PLANNING JOB IS MUCH BIGGER THAN I THOUGHT IT WAS. I WANTED TO DO IT ON MY OWN, BUT IT WAS A GOOD IDEA TO ASK YOU TO COME.
BUT NOW I'M WORRIED THAT IT'S A LITTLE MUCH, EVEN FOR YOU. WOULD YOU... WOULD YOU LIKE ME TO ASK CHEESE SANDWICH TO HELP OUT, TOO?

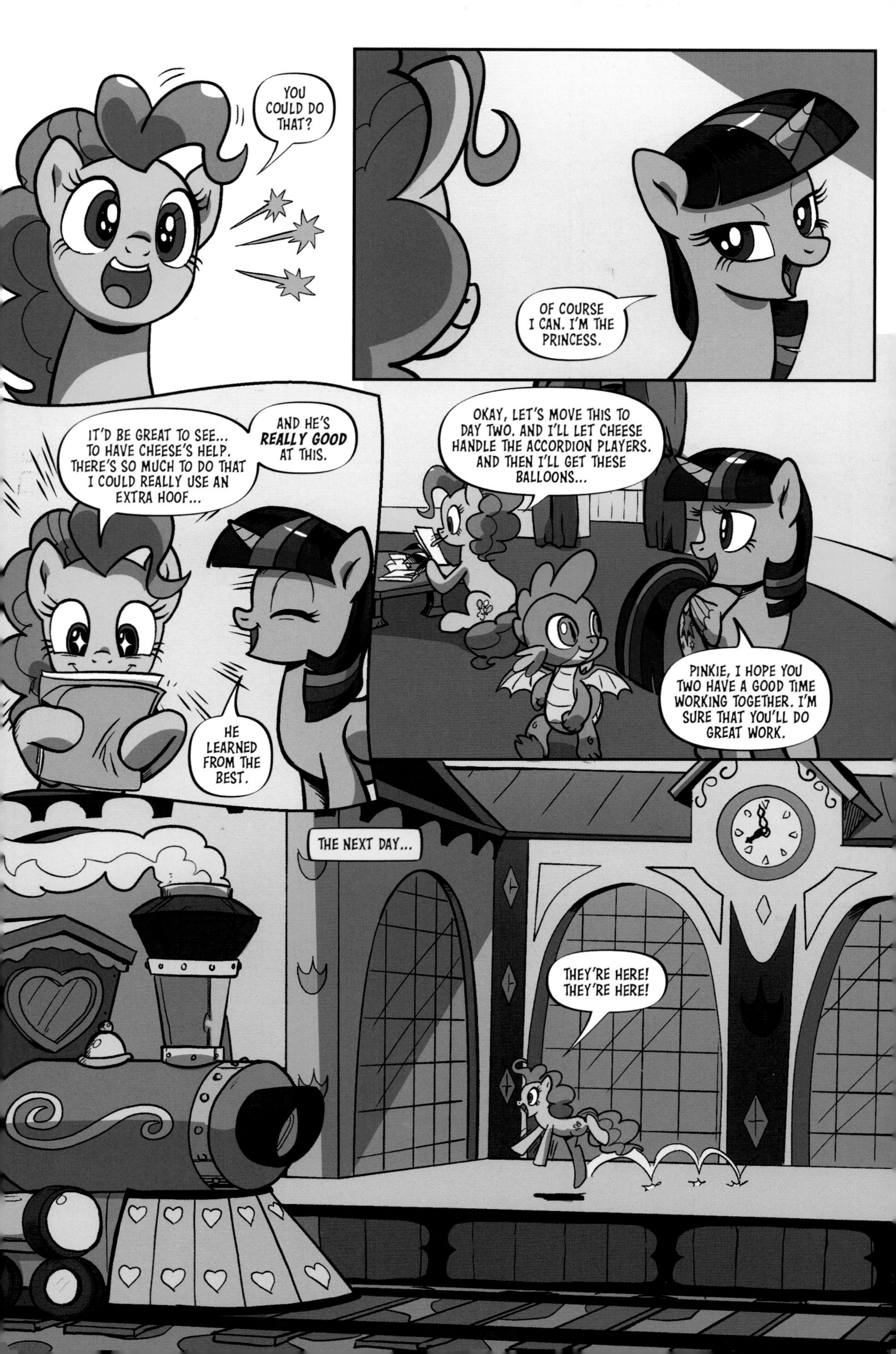
YOU COULD DO THAT?
OF COURSE I CAN. I'M THE PRINCESS.
IT'D BE GREAT TO SEE... TO HAVE CHEESE'S HELP. THERE'S SO MUCH TO DO THAT I COULD REALLY USE AN EXTRA HOOF...
AND HE'S **REALLY GOOD** AT THIS.
HE LEARNED FROM THE BEST.
OKAY, LET'S MOVE THIS TO DAY TWO. AND I'LL LET CHEESE HANDLE THE ACCORDION PLAYERS. AND THEN I'LL GET THESE BALLOONS...
PINKIE, I HOPE YOU TWO HAVE A GOOD TIME WORKING TOGETHER. I'M SURE THAT YOU'LL DO GREAT WORK.
THE NEXT DAY...
THEY'RE HERE! THEY'RE HERE!

WELCOME! GOOD TO SEE--

--OH, IT'S YOU.
WELL, THAT'S A FINE WELCOME FOR THE LEADER OF THE WONDERBOLTS FLYING SQUAD FOR THE FESTIVAL.
SORRY. I JUST WASN'T EXPECTING YOU.

OH, THERE YOU ARE!
?

--OH.
--THAT'S RIGHT, I WANT THE THIRTY CASES OF CIDER DELIVERED TO THE CASTLE.
OH, HI, PINKIE.

THERE?

--OH.
PINKIE, DARLING, HOW SWEET OF YOU TO SEE ME ARRIVE! I FEEL SO SPECIAL.

NOW. FINALLY?

--AND THEN THE BUTTERFLIES WILL ARRIVE.
BRILLIANT!
HELLO, PLINKIE.
5
IT'S PINKIE!

AND SINCE WHEN DO YOU RIDE TRAINS?!

HE SAID HE WANTS TO SEE HOW THE COMMON CREATURES TRAVELED.
ALSO, HE LIKES CHOO-CHOO TRAINS, APPARENTLY.
CHEESE! YOU'RE HERE!
CRACK
I AM.
THANKS! THAT WORKED OUT THE KINK IN MY BACK.
GOOD TO SEE YOU, PINKIE.
GOOD TO SEE YOU, TOO.
SO, I HEAR YOU'VE GOT A PARTY TO PLAN.
NO. *WE'VE* GOT A PARTY TO PLAN.

PRINCESS TWILIGHT GAVE US A LOT TO WORK WITH. IT'S A SOLID START.
SHE DID, BUT FOR GOODNESS' SAKE, DON'T TELL THAT TO HER.
LONG STORY.
WE CAN HAVE STILT WALKERS IN COSTUME WALKING AROUND THE CROWD AND HANDING OUT CANDY. DEFINITELY CANDY!
AND WE COULD HAVE A T-SHIRT STAND HERE. AND MAYBE LITTLE PLASTIC FIGURINES. AND--
--AND--
SHIRTS
HUH.
MAYBE WE CAN CALL THEM ***PEPS!*** PLASTIC EQUESTRIAN PONIES!
OH, YEAH. THEY'LL JUST POP OFF THE SHELVES.

I'M REALLY GLAD YOU HAD TWILIGHT SUMMON ME--
IT WASN'T REALLY A SUMMONS--
TWO DRAGONS DELIVERED ME A SCROLL. IT WAS A SUMMONS.
BUT I WOULD HAVE COME EVEN IF IT WAS JUST A POSTCARD. I'M ALWAYS GLAD TO SEE YOU. AND I WANTED TO ASK... TO ASK--
--TO ASK WHAT THE HECK IS THAT?!
I DON'T KNOW. MAYBE TWILIGHT COMMISSIONED A POOL?
IT'S A SINK HOLE. THERE ARE ALL THOSE CAVERNS THAT RUN UNDERNEATH THE CITY. ONE OF THEM GAVE IN.
EXPO POSITION
WE'LL HAVE IT SHORED UP BY THE FESTIVAL, BUT FOR NOW, STAY BACK.
THOSE THINGS CAN BE DANGEROUS.
DANGEROUS AND--
--PERFECT.
EXPO POSITION

I DIDN'T EVEN THINK ABOUT THE CAVES. I SHOULD HAVE, BECAUSE I'VE BEEN IN THEM BEFORE.
THERE'S A WHOLE NETWORK--AND SOME OF THEM ARE PRETTY CLOSE TO THE SURFACE.
WE COULD PUT SOME SPEAKERS DOWN HERE. REALLY PUMP THE BASS.
WE COULD RIG UP SOME SPOTLIGHTS DOWN HERE, TOO. SHOOT COLUMNS OF COLOR INTO THE AIR DURING SOME OF THE CONCERTS. MAYBE TWILIGHT'S INEVITABLE SPEECH.
WANT TO SEE WHAT OTHER TROUBLE WE COULD GET INTO?
ABSOLUTELY!

SO, YOU'VE BEEN DOWN HERE BEFORE?
YEAH, STARSWIRL USED TO DO SOME PROJECTS DOWN HERE.
BUT LET'S STAY AWAY FROM ANYTHING THAT LOOKS STRANGE OR MAGICAL. WE SHOULD JUST CONCENTRATE ON THINGS WE CAN USE FOR THE FESTIVAL.

OKAY.
WHAT ARE YOU DOING?

WELL, YOU'RE BOTH STRANGE AND MAGICAL. SO I'M KEEPING MY DISTANCE AND TRYING TO KEEP FROM LOOKING DIRECTLY AT YOU.

AND YOU ARE THE BEST KIND OF SILLY--
--WAIT, CHEESE, WATCH OUT!

WHOOPS!
GOTCHA!
YEAH--
--YOU DO.
COME ON. LET'S GET BACK UP TOP. I THINK WE'VE SEEN EVERYTHING WE NEED TO.
AND THEN YOU CAN TELL EVERYPONY ABOUT YOUR NICE TRIP.
IT WAS MOSTLY ***FALL-DEROL.***
I CAN'T TAKE THIS ***PUN-ISHMENT.***

MEANWHILE--
RAINBOW DASH AND HER CADETS ARE SO MUCH FUN TO WATCH.
YOU KNOW, YOU CAN FLY TOO.
YEAH, BUT NOT LIKE THAT.
WHAT'S WRONG, DISCORD?
IT'S JUST SO HARD BEING GOOD! THERE'S NOTHING TO DO. NOTHING TO MAKE.

THAT'S NOT TRUE.

I ASKED TWILIGHT FOR A BUNCH OF ART SUPPLIES. WE NEED TO MAKE SIGNS FOR THE PETTING ZOO. I COULD USE SOME HELP.

SEE! THIS IS FUN.
REALLY? WITH ONE SNAP OF MY FINGERS, I COULD JUST MAKE THESE SIGNS APPEAR.
THEY'D EVEN DANCE! MAYBE HAVE SOME PONY SPINNING IT AROUND ACROBATICALLY.
WHICH, OF COURSE, I WOULDN'T DO, BECAUSE THE IMPORTANT PART IS DOING THINGS FOR OURSELVES.
EXACTLY.

COULD I HAVE THE GREEN PAINT, PLEASE?

--AND THEN MAYBE WE CAN PUT YOUR PARTY CANNON DOWN THERE, TOO.
THAT'S A GREAT IDEA! IT'LL BE PART OF OUR BIG FINALE!
THIS IS GOING TO BE THE BEST FESTIVAL OF THE TWO SISTERS EVER!
SPROING!
IT WAS FUN EXPLORING THOSE CAVES WITH YOU, PINKIE. WE DO GO TO THE MOST INTERESTING PLACES AND HAVE THE BEST ADVENTURES.
TRAVEL'S ALWAYS BETTER WITH A FRIEND.
WE COULD HAVE ONE OF THE BANDS PLAY IN FRONT OF THIS REFLECTING POOL, TOO.

WHY, LOOK AT THOSE TWO AMAZINGLY GOOD-LOOKING PONIES!

HEY!
SPLASH!

WHAT WAS THAT FOR?
YOU LOOKED LIKE YOU WERE GETTING TOO LOST IN THOUGHT. THAT'S NO GOOD.
PLUS IT WAS FUNNY.

IT WAS!

OH, HEY, I SEE A GREAT PLACE FOR AN ICE CREAM STAND!
NOW I WANT ICE CREAM! I LOVE ROCKY ROAD!

YOU COMING?
I'LL BE ALONG IN A MINUTE. THIS REFLECTION IS PRETTY CUTE.
I JUST NEED A BREAK.
SURE!
SIGH
YOU COULD JUST SAY SOMETHING, YOU KNOW.

RIGHT, LIKE IT'S THAT EASY!
WHY DIDN'T **YOU** JUST SAY SOMETHING?

I WOULD, BUT I'M JUST IN YOUR HEAD, PINKAMENA. YOU NEED TO DO THIS. YOU **WANT** TO DO THIS.

BUT I DON'T WANT TO SAY ANYTHING. I MEAN, I DO, BUT I DON'T.
I'M WORRIED.
YOU? WORRIED? REALLY? THAT'S WEIRD.
NORMALLY YOU JUST BLURT EVERYTHING OUT! THERE'S NOT A LOT OF THOUGHT. WHY IS THIS ONE STUCK IN OUR HEAD?
BECAUSE THIS IS IMPORTANT.
PINKIE, COME HERE! YOU HAVE TO SEE WHAT'S HAPPENING!
GO ON. GO. JUST SAY SOMETHING, OKAY?
YEAH. I WILL.

CHEESE, I WANT TO TELL YOU

?!
?!
Bags & sacks
To be contin

The Muffletta: a History.
From the journals of Starswirl the Bearded
SORTS OF FLORA
VOL.8

THE
TROOF!
YE OLDE TOME

THE
TROOF!
YE OLDE TOME

THE MUFFLETTA
A MAGIC MOSS THAT ABSORBS SOUND
IN SMALL QUANTITIES IT KEEPS THINGS QUIET!
WITH SUNLIGHT AND WATER, IT MULTIPLIES!!!
COMFORT
HOW DO WE STOP IT???
WE DON'T KNOW!!!

CONFUSION
IDEA

EFFORT
DEFEAT

CHAOS
NOD
Bothersome botanical burdens

PANIC
CATCH
PLEAD
PLEAD
!

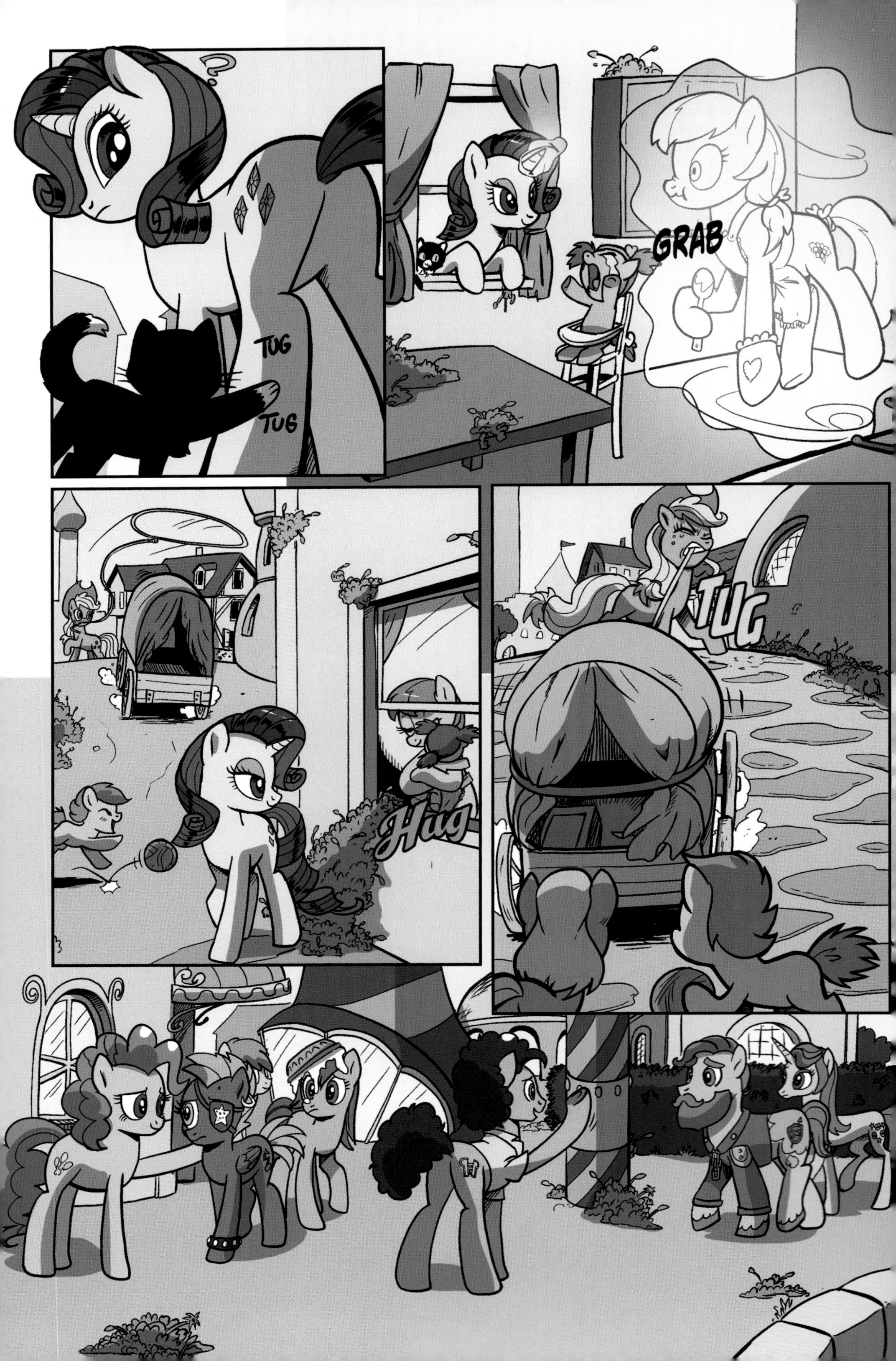
?
TUG
TUG
GRAB
Hug
TUG

WHAT IS GOING ON ?
WHAT IS GOING ON
SAD

TOUCH
CONNECT

-AHAHAHAHAH
AHAHAHAH
AHAHAHAH
AHAH
?
?

HARD THINKING
BREAD
DOUGH

HA
HA
HA
HA
HA
HA

—AHAHHAHHA!

INTENSITY

HEE HAHAHA
HEE HEE!
HEEHEEHAHEE

SNICKER!
HAH HAH!
SHRINK SHRINK
JUGGLE
BALANCE
HEH HEE HEE
BWHA HAH HAH
HA HA HA HA HA HA
HO HO
HA HA HA HA HA HA HA HA HA HA HA HA
HO HO HO
BWHA HAH HAH HAH
HAH HAH HAH

HA
HEE
HA HA HA
HA HA
HEE
HA HA HA HA
HA
HA HA HA HA
HA HA HA HA
HA HA HA HAH
HA HA HA HA HA HA HA HA HA
HA HAH HAH HA HA HA HA HA
HA HA HA HA HA
SCIENCE
HAH
HAH
HAH

MATH
HA
HA
HA
HA
F=c/2
IS GIGGLE THE ANSWER?
POLLEN? LAUGH!?
MAYBE A LOT OF FIRE!?
HA HA HAH HA HAH
TOSS THE MOSS!
LAUGHTER IS THE BEST MEDICINE
ROYAL COMMAND PERFORMANCE
(I COMMAND YOU TO ATTEND)
(PLEASE)

A FEW HOURS LATER...
--IT'S ALMOST FITTING THAT TODAY, OF ALL DAYS, THE SOUND OF LAUGHTER--*GENUINE* LAUGHTER--WAS THE SOLUTION TO OUR PROBLEMS.
WHEN THEY WERE FOALS, THE TWO SISTERS CELESTIA AND LUNA BONDED WITH LAUGHTER.
AND IT'S LAUGHTER, THE SOUND OF FRIENDSHIP, THAT WE CELEBRATE TODAY.
SHARED MOMENTS AND SHARED JOKES ARE PART OF RELATIONSHIPS, FROM SISTERS TO BROTHERS TO PARENTS TO FRIENDS AND EVERYTHING IN BETWEEN.
DISCORD!
WHERE WERE YOU? WHEN THE MUFFLETTA SILENCED EVERYTHING, YOU DISAPPEARED! WE COULD HAVE USED YOUR HELP.
YOU SAID, "DOING THINGS FOR OURSELVES IS IMPORTANT."
SO, I LET YOU DO FOR YOURSELVES.

BESIDES, IT WAS FUNNIER.
UNLIKE THIS PART OF THE SPEECH. THIS IS ALL PADDING.
LAUGHTER IS THE MORTAR IN THE BRICKS OF FRIENDSHIP.

THAT WAS PRETTY FRIGHTENING. I CAN'T BELIEVE THAT I BROUGHT THAT MOSS TOPSIDE.
IT WAS AN ACCIDENT. ANYPONY COULD HAVE DONE IT.

I WAS AFRAID FOR A WHILE I'D NEVER HEAR ANYTHING AGAIN.
AND THEN WE DID. AND IT WAS THE BEST SOUND IN THE WORLD.

OUR LAUGHTER.

DON'T GET ME WRONG. I HAVE A DELIGHTFUL LAUGH ON MY OWN.
BUT IT'S EVEN BETTER WHEN YOU'RE LAUGHING WITH ME.
BEST SOUND IN THE WORLD.

I DON'T KNOW IF YOU NOTICED, BUT I'VE BEEN A LITTLE WEIRD AROUND YOU LATELY.
NOT MY NORMAL WEIRD, BUT WEIRD-WEIRD.

I NOTICED. I'VE BEEN WEIRD, TOO. WEIRD-WEIRD. NOT WEIRD-WEIRD-WEIRD, IF YOU KNOW--
--WELL, YOU'RE PINKIE. YOU KNOW.

I KEPT TRYING TO SAY THINGS TO YOU, BUT THE WORDS GOT IN THE WAY.
WELL, AND THEN THE WORDS WENT AWAY COMPLETELY.
LAUGHING WITH YOU... THAT'S EVERYTHING I WAS TRYING TO SAY.

I LOVE LAUGHING WITH YOU. AND OUR LAUGHS ARE JUST BETTER TOGETHER.
NOT JUST BETTER. THEY'RE THE BEST.

YOU KNOW, THIS WAS QUIET AN ADVENTURE WE HAD.
THAT'S A SOUND OBSERVATION, CHEESE.
HAHAHAHAHAHAH!
Fin
The End!

THE TWO KINGDOMS OF CANINIA

OH, BIG MAAA-AAAC? DO YOU THINK YOU COULD WATCH THE BUMPS?
IT REALLY IS DIFFICULT TO KNIT WHEN THE CART KEEPS BUMPING UP AND DOWN.
YOU WOULDN'T WANT TO RUIN ONE OF MY LOVELY SWEATERS, WOULD YOU?
SIGH
NOPE.
I HATE TO SEEM ORNERY, BUT I AIN'T REALLY SURE WHY AN EMISSARY TO THE PRINCESS IS KNITTING SWEATERS AT ALL.
SEEMS LIKE MAYBE WE OUGHTTA BE TRYING TO FIGURE OUT WHY WE GOT TWO ROYAL INVITATIONS FOR TWO DIFFERENT QUEENS!
MEADOWBROOK, DARLING, I'M SURE THAT'S JUST A MISTAKE.
AS FOR THE SWEATERS, WE'RE EMISSARIES TO A RACE OF DOG PEOPLE WHO HAVE TONS OF VERY EXPENSIVE ROCKS.
AND IF THERE'S ANYTHING I KNOW ABOUT DOGS, IT'S THAT THEY NEED CUTE SWEATERS. AND PERHAPS WE COULD ARRANGE A AHEM TRADE.
AND SINCE WE HAVE MAUD ALONG TO EVALUATE THOSE ROCKS... WHERE IS MAUD ANYWAY?
GANGWAY!

BOOM
BOULDER SAID HE HEARD YOU CALLING FOR ME.
MY GOODNESS, MAUD! WHERE HAVE YOU BEEN? DISCOVERING SOMETHING SHINY AND EXPENSIVE, I HOPE.
NO. BUT BOULDER AND I HAVE MADE SEVERAL IMPORTANT GEOLOGICAL DISCOVERIES. THEY WILL KEEP ME WRITING PAPERS FOR YEARS. I'M VERY EXCITED.
OH! WELL, TO EACH THEIR OWN, I SUPPOSE. OOH! SPEAKING OF OUR NEW CANINE FRIENDS, I THINK WE'RE HERE.
HELLOOOO! MY NAME IS RARITY, AND I AM AN EMISSARY FROM PRINCESS TWILIGHT SPARKLE OF EQUESTRIA.
GO CAR. GO CAR GO.
SO... WE SHOULD TAKE THE CABLE CAR THEN?
MINE. MINE CAR.
THE CAR IS YOURS? IT'S VERY NICE. KIND OF A STRANGE CABLE CAR.
THAT'S BECAUSE IT'S NOT A CABLE CAR. IT'S A MINE CAR.

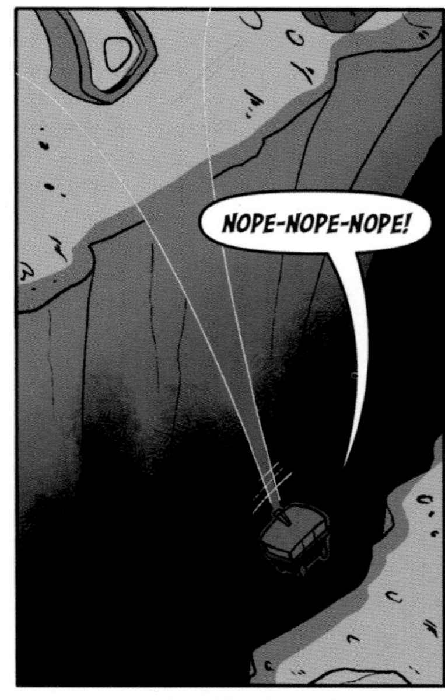
NOPE-NOPE-NOPE!

AAAAAAHHHHH!

WHOOOOOOOA!

YAAAAAAHHHH!

OOOOOOOH!

CLACK
HUH?

I DISLIKED THAT TREMENDOUSLY.
YUP.
AGREED!
IT WAS FINE. NOW LOOK AT THAT.

WOW. TWO COMPLETELY SEPARATE CASTLES. THINK THAT MIGHT HAVE SOMETHING TO DO WITH THE TWO INVITATIONS?
NOW, MEADOWBROOK, SMUG SELF-SATISFACTION IS VERY OUT THIS SEASON.

GREETINGS TO YOU, EMISSARIES FROM EQUESTRIA. WE HAVE BEEN AWAITING YOUR ARRIVAL.
WELCOME TO CANINIA!

I'M **PRINCESS MOONBEAM TWINKLETAIL**, BUT YOU CAN JUST CALL ME MOON.
AND THIS IS MY SISTER--
WHO CAN INTRODUCE HERSELF.

I AM **PRINCESS AMBROSIA MUFFINBUNS**, PLEASE CALL ME AMBER.
AND TELL ME, WHO ARE YOU, AND WHO DOES YOUR MANE? IS EVERYPONY IN EQUESTRIA SO WELL-COIFFED?
I AM RARITY, AND THEY WISH!

I HAD NO IDEA I WOULD MEET A DIAMOND DOG WITH SO MUCH FASHION SENSE.
TO BE FRANK, THE DIAMOND DOGS I'VE MET IN EQUESTRIA HAVE BEEN--
THEY'RE VERY DISTANT COUSINS. I LOVE THEM, BUT FASHION IS NOT THEIR FORTE.

WELL, LOOKS LIKE THEY'RE GONNA BE GOOD FRIENDS.
THE REST OF YOU CAN COME WITH ME. LET'S GO SEE MY SISTER, THE QUEEN.

VISITORS! IT'S BEEN SO LONG SINCE I'VE HAD VISITORS!
PLEASE, JENN, DON'T STRAIN YOURSELF. BE CAREFUL.
NONSENSE, MOON. I AM--

OOH!
SISTER!

THAT WAS EMBARRASSING.
IT'S OKAY, GO SLOW.
THANK YOU, MOON.

I AM ***QUEEN JENNINO LANTERNLIGHT***, BUT THAT IS SUCH A MOUTHFUL.
JENN WILL BE JUST FINE.
NOW, TELL ME, HOW WAS YOUR TRIP HERE? I USED TO GO OUTSIDE ALL THE TIME, BUT SINCE MY ILLNESS, I BARELY GET OUT.

WELL, YOUR VALLEY REALLY IS LOVELY.
AND THE RIDE IN IS... SOMETHING ELSE.
YUP.

AH, THE GO CAR! I LOVE THOSE THINGS. WE USE THEM ALL AROUND THE KINGDOM.
UMM... RARITY?
SHOULD WE ASK ABOUT THE TWO INVITATIONS? ONE SAYS QUEEN JENNINO, BUT THE OTHER ONE--
THERE'S PLENTY OF TIME FOR THAT. IT WOULD BE VERY RUDE TO BUTT IN RIGHT NOW.
WE REALLY ARE EXCITED TO BEGIN THIS NEW ALLIANCE. WE'VE HEARD SO MANY STORIES ABOUT PRINCESS TWILIGHT--
--AND WE HAVE SO FEW TRADE PARTNERS. TELL ME, RARITY...
DO YOU LIKE DIAMONDS? BECAUSE WE HAVE A LOT OF THEM.
I THINK I'M IN LOVE.
I WISH I COULD SHOW YOU THE KINGDOM, BUT AS YOU CAN SEE, GETTING AROUND IS QUITE DIFFICULT FOR ME.
MY SISTERS WILL GIVE YOU A TOUR OF THE CASTLE AND GROUNDS, AND THEN TONIGHT WE FEAST!
WE'RE SPARING NO EXPENSE FOR OUR GUESTS.

THIS IS THE MAGIC LIBRARY MY SISTER BOUGHT FOR ME TO STUDY. IT'S FULL OF BOOKS ON SPELLS AND POTIONS.

THIS IS THE ROYAL SPA, MY SISTER'S PRESENT TO ME.
NOW THAT *IS* QUITE THE PRESENT!

THIS IS THE QUEEN LANTERNLIGHT ACADEMY. ALL PUPPIES CAN COME AND LEARN FROM THE ROYAL TUTORS.
THE ROYAL ACADEMY IS OPEN TO ALL? IMPRESSIVE.

AND THESE ARE THE GARDENS WHERE WE GROW--
GOLDEN APPLES?!

RARITY!
AMBROSIA, DARLING, I HATE TO INTER-RUUUPT, BUT...
OKAY, OKAY.

...WHAT AM I LOOKING AT?
OH... WELL...
THAT'S THE **OTHER** KINGDOM OF CANINIA.

THERE ARE TWO?
YES, AND IT'S ACTUALLY RUN BY OUR... OTHER OLDER SISTER.

HOW MANY OF YOU ARE THERE?
SIX IN ALL, THOUGH WE HAVEN'T SEEN OUR OTHER THREE SISTERS IN...

YEARS! IT'S BEEN **YEARS** SINCE I'VE SEEN FIONA!
THEY'RE TWINS. SHE GETS VERY SENSITIVE ABOUT IT.

I CANNOT BLAME HER. IF I HAD TO GO THAT LONG WITHOUT SEEING MY SISTERS, I WOULD BE VERY EMOTIONAL, TOO.
RARITY, WE HAVE TO DO SOMETHING.

HOW DID THIS HAPPEN?

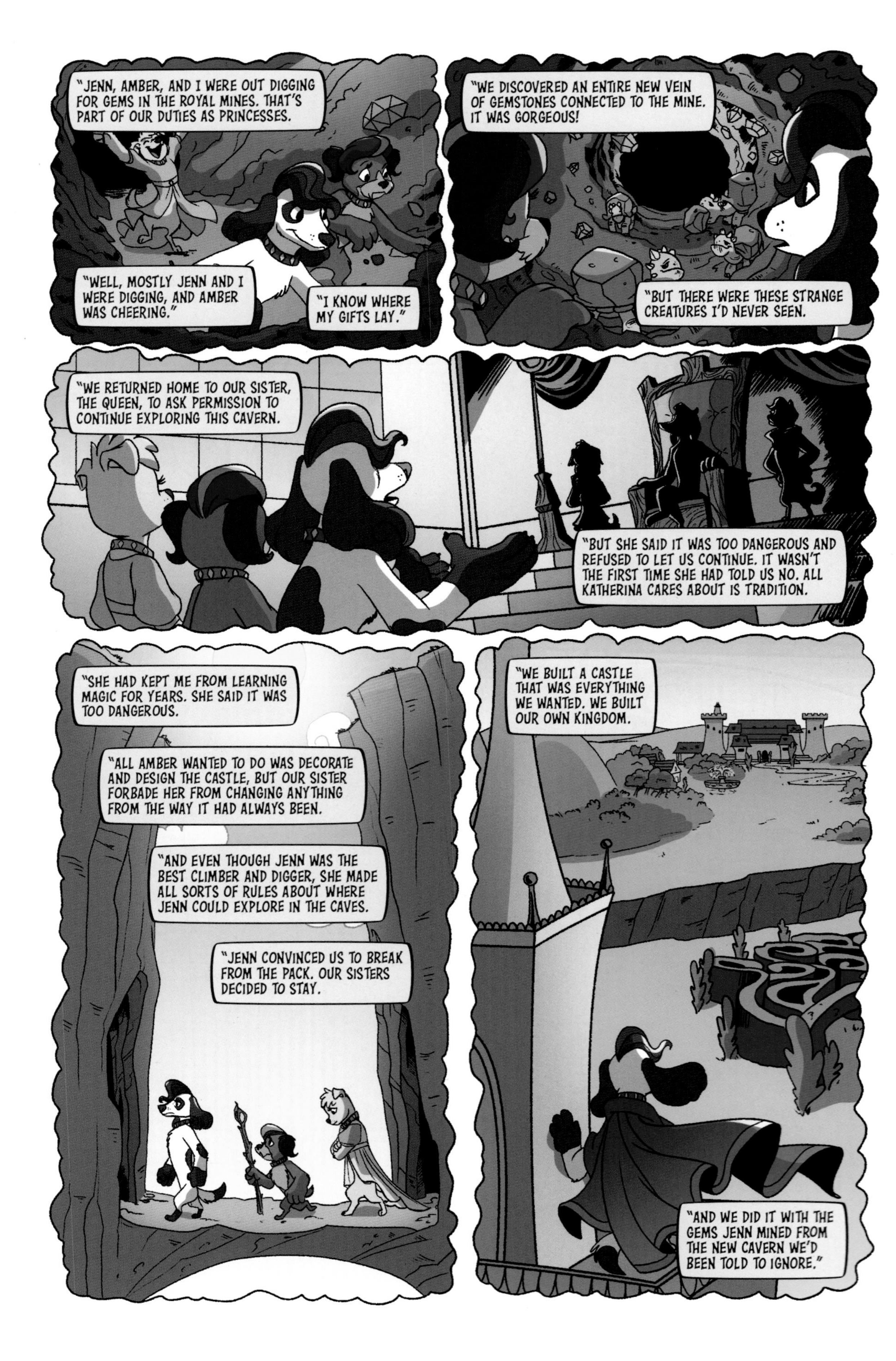
"JENN, AMBER, AND I WERE OUT DIGGING FOR GEMS IN THE ROYAL MINES. THAT'S PART OF OUR DUTIES AS PRINCESSES.
"WELL, MOSTLY JENN AND I WERE DIGGING, AND AMBER WAS CHEERING."
"I KNOW WHERE MY GIFTS LAY."
"WE DISCOVERED AN ENTIRE NEW VEIN OF GEMSTONES CONNECTED TO THE MINE. IT WAS GORGEOUS!
"BUT THERE WERE THESE STRANGE CREATURES I'D NEVER SEEN.
"WE RETURNED HOME TO OUR SISTER, THE QUEEN, TO ASK PERMISSION TO CONTINUE EXPLORING THIS CAVERN.
"BUT SHE SAID IT WAS TOO DANGEROUS AND REFUSED TO LET US CONTINUE. IT WASN'T THE FIRST TIME SHE HAD TOLD US NO. ALL KATHERINA CARES ABOUT IS TRADITION.
"SHE HAD KEPT ME FROM LEARNING MAGIC FOR YEARS. SHE SAID IT WAS TOO DANGEROUS.
"ALL AMBER WANTED TO DO WAS DECORATE AND DESIGN THE CASTLE, BUT OUR SISTER FORBADE HER FROM CHANGING ANYTHING FROM THE WAY IT HAD ALWAYS BEEN.
"AND EVEN THOUGH JENN WAS THE BEST CLIMBER AND DIGGER, SHE MADE ALL SORTS OF RULES ABOUT WHERE JENN COULD EXPLORE IN THE CAVES.
"JENN CONVINCED US TO BREAK FROM THE PACK. OUR SISTERS DECIDED TO STAY.
"WE BUILT A CASTLE THAT WAS EVERYTHING WE WANTED. WE BUILT OUR OWN KINGDOM.
"AND WE DID IT WITH THE GEMS JENN MINED FROM THE NEW CAVERN WE'D BEEN TOLD TO IGNORE."

BUT THEN JENN GOT SICK, AND KATHERINA REFUSED TO LET OUR SISTERS COME VISIT.
SHE SAID IT WAS JENN'S OWN STUBBORNNESS THAT HAD MADE HER ILL.

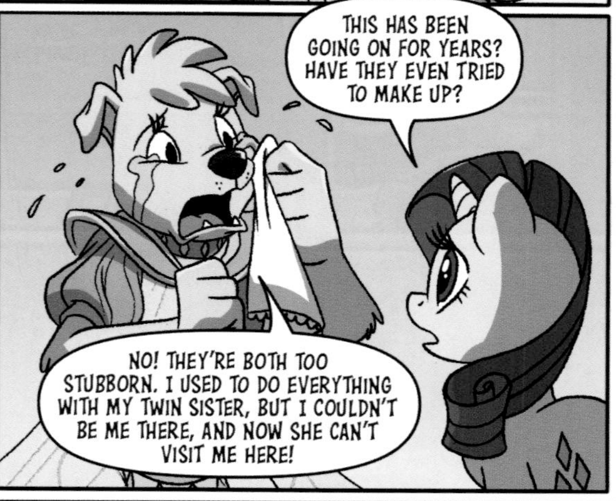

THIS HAS BEEN GOING ON FOR YEARS? HAVE THEY EVEN TRIED TO MAKE UP?
NO! THEY'RE BOTH TOO STUBBORN. I USED TO DO EVERYTHING WITH MY TWIN SISTER, BUT I COULDN'T BE ME THERE, AND NOW SHE CAN'T VISIT ME HERE!

YOU ALL ARE IN LUCK. FIXING FRIENDSHIPS IS RARITY'S SPECIALTY.
MY SPECIALTY IS ROCKS.
WELL... I WOULD SAY BETWEEN MAUD, BIG MAC, AND I, WE'VE DEALT WITH QUITE A FEW CONFLICTS BETWEEN SISTERS.

WE WILL VISIT THE OTHER CASTLE AND SEE IF WE CAN SORT THIS OUT.
NOW, HOW DO WE GET THERE?

I MISS WALKING! I NEVER THOUGHT I'D MISS WALKING!

AAAAAAHHHHHHH!

REGRETTING EATING ALL OF THOSE APPLES NOW?
YUP.

YAY, VISITORS!
I'M **PRINCESS FIONA FLOPPYEARS**, AND THIS IS MY SISTER, **PRINCESS INDIANA EMBEREYES**.
CALL US FIONA AND INDY. IT'S A PLEASURE TO MAKE YOUR ACQUAINTANCE! WE WEREN'T SURE YOU GOT OUR INVITATION.

YES, WELL... THERE WAS A BIT OF A MIXUP WITH THE INVITATIONS.
I'M RARITY AND... WAIT, FIONA, YOU'RE AMBER'S TWIN?
YOU ALL DON'T SEEM LIKE--

--LIKE WE'VE BEEN APART FOR A DAY? LIKE WE'VE BEEN WITHOUT EACH OTHER FOR SO LONG? LIKE YOU COULD EVEN TELL US APART?!
HOW IS AMBIE? I LOVE MY TWIN SO MUCH, BUT I UNDERSTAND THAT SHE HAD TO LEAVE TO DO WHAT SHE LOVED. SOMETIMES I WISH I'D GONE WITH HER, BUT I COULDN'T LEAVE INDY ALONE. ARE WE STILL JUST ALIKE?

YOU'RE JUST THE SPITTING IMAGE OF ONE ANOTHER.
I KNEW IT! I JUST KNEW IT! DID YOU HEAR THAT, INDY?

NOW, FIONA SAID SHE DIDN'T WANT TO LEAVE YOU ALONE, BUT I THOUGHT...?
MY OLDER SISTER TAKES BEING QUEEN VERY SERIOUSLY. IT'S HER SACRED DUTY. IT DOESN'T LEAVE TIME FOR MUCH ELSE.
SPEAKING OF WHICH, SHE'LL BE WAITING. WE SHOULD GO.

SO... FIONA, DO YOU DO ANY OF THE DECORATING IN THE HOUSE?
OH, NO. OUR SISTER SAYS WE'RE TO LEAVE EVERYTHING THE SAME AS IT HAS ALWAYS BEEN. EVEN IF IT IS KINDA DARK AND DEPRESSING.
I DO TRY TO MAKE HER LAUGH WHEN I CAN THOUGH! I GOT A CHUCKLE FROM HER EARLIER THIS WEEK.

SEEMS MORE LIKE A PRISON THAN A HOME.
YUP.

HERE WE ARE.
THIS IS THE THRONE ROOM?
INDEED. AND ALLOW ME TO INTRODUCE YOU TO...

QUEEN KATHERINA PROUDPAWS, REGENT OF CANINIA AND PROTECTOR OF THE SACRED MINES OF OUR ANCESTORS.
YOU ARE WELCOME TO REFER TO ME AS--
LET ME GUESS! KAT?
GASP
YOU MAY NOT!
AND THAT WORD IS FORBIDDEN IN THIS KINGDOM, SO I WOULD MIND YOUR TONGUE!
OH, I'M SO SORRY. I'LL LET YOU FINISH.
YOU MAY REFER TO ME AS "YOUR MAJESTY" OR "YOUR ROYAL HIGHNESS," AS HAS BEEN TRADITION IN THIS KINGDOM SINCE MY GREAT-GREAT-GRANDMOTHER SAT ON THIS VERY THRONE. TRADITION IS VERY IMPORTANT.
OF COURSE! APOLOGIES, YOUR MAJESTY.
THAT IS MORE LIKE IT. NOW, HOW MAY I ASSIST THE EMISSARY OF EQUESTRIA?

WELL... YOUR MAJESTY... WE WANTED TO ESTABLISH A FRIENDLY RELATIONSHIP BETWEEN CANINIA AND EQUESTRIA.
BUT... WELL... IT SEEMS THERE ARE TWO KINGDOMS OF CANINIA.
I AM THE ONLY RIGHTFUL QUEEN, AND WHO IS TO SAY THAT I WISH TO MAKE A TREATY WITH EQUESTRIA?
IT SEEMS YOUR KINGDOM IS ALWAYS EMBROILED IN SOME CONFLICT.
THE MOST IMPORTANT THING TO ME IS THE SAFETY OF MY SUBJECTS.
I HAVE FIVE YOUNGER SIBLINGS THAT COUNT ON MY PROTECTION, AND I WILL NOT BE TRICKED INTO ENDANGERING THEM SIMPLY TO MAKE NEW FRIENDS.
IF YOUR SISTERS ARE SO IMPORTANT TO YOU, WHY HAVEN'T YOU EVEN ALLOWED THEM TO VISIT EACH OTHER?
THE TWINS HAVEN'T SEEN EACH OTHER IN YEARS, AND YOU USE THEM AS AN EXCUSE?
YUP!
HOW DARE YOU?!
PRINCESS JENNINO LANTERNLIGHT MADE THE CHOICE TO ENDANGER HERSELF AND OUR SISTERS, AND BECAUSE OF HER GREED, SHE FELL ILL.
I DO NOT ALLOW MY TWO LOYAL SISTERS TO VISIT BECAUSE THEY MAY BECOME VICTIMS OF THAT GREED AS WELL.
WHAT IF THEY GOT SICK? WHERE WOULD THE FUTURE OF OUR COUNTRY BE THEN?
MY SISTER THINKS THE ONLY WAY TO RUN A COUNTRY IS TO LET HEIRS TO THE THRONE DO WHATEVER THEY LIKE.
AND SO, THEY DECORATE, AND USE MAGIC RECKLESSLY, AND DIG WHEREVER THEY LIKE WITH NO REGARD FOR SAFETY. THEN THEY CALL ME THE MEAN ONE.

BUT I AM NOT MEAN. I AM *LOYAL*.
MY DEAR PARENTS ENTRUSTED THE SAFETY OF MY SISTERS TO ME. I CANNOT STOP JENN FROM ENDANGERING HERSELF, BUT I WILL STOP HER FROM ENDANGERING OUR ENTIRE KINGDOM!
SHE COULD MAKE THEM ALL SICK!

WHAT IF WE COULD DETERMINE WHAT MADE YOUR SISTER SICK? MAYBE EVEN CURE IT?
AND HOW WOULD YOU DO THAT?

I'M MAGE MEADOWBROOK. I DARE SAY IF THERE'S ANY CREATURE THAT'S KNOWN FOR HEALIN' PONYFOLK, IT'S ME.
I THINK I CAN UNCOVER THE SOURCE O' WHAT MADE JENN SICK, AND I COULD BE SURE NO ONE *ELSE* GETS SICK!

YOU WOULD PUT YOURSELF AT RISK FOR MY SISTERS?
I'D TAKE PRECAUTIONS, BUT I'VE GONE INTO TIGHTER SPOTS TO HELP A PONY OUT.

VERY WELL. MY SISTERS AND I SHALL ESCORT YOU TO THE EDGE OF THE MINE, AND YOU ALL WILL ATTEMPT TO DISCOVER THE SOURCE OF THE ILLNESS.
BUT I WARN YOU, IF SOMETHING HAPPENS TO YOU THERE, WE WILL NOT COME IN AFTER YOU.
UNDERSTOOD.

WHAT ARE **THEY** DOING HERE?
WE SAW OUR NEW FRIENDS WERE GOING INTO THE MINES.
IF THERE WAS TROUBLE, WE KNEW THEY WOULD NEED BACKUP. AFTER ALL, **YOU'RE** NOT GOING TO GO IN AND HELP THEM.
HARUMPH!
WELL, I HAVE TO SAY, I DID NOT EXPECT TO BE LOWERED INTO A TERRIFYING PIT ON THIS MISSION.
I'M CONFIDENT THAT BETWEEN MY KNOWLEDGE OF TOXINS AND MAUD'S KNOWLEDGE OF GEOLOGY, WE'LL FIGURE THIS OUT.
YUP.

HEY!
OH, I'M SORRY, DO YOU OWN "YUP"?
IT SEEMS THEY'RE CLOSER NOW THAN THEY'VE BEEN IN SOME TIME.
AT LEAST PHYSICALLY.

THIS IS WHERE JENN SAID THE NEW CAVERN WAS. SHE MADE IT SOUND LIKE A TIGHTER SPACE, THOUGH.
IT LOOKS LIKE THEY HAVE BEEN MINING IN HERE FOR DECADES.
YUP.

IT ONLY LOOKS LIKE MINING FROM A DISTANCE. BUT LOOK AT THESE GROOVES.
WHAT ARE THEY?
BITE MARKS.

FROM THAT GUY.
OH, HOW ADORABLE. IT'S A LITTLE ROCK TURTLE!

WHOA, HEAVY LITTLE FELLA.
HE SHOULD BE. HE'S A ***CARBUNKAPPA***, AND HE'S BEEN FILLING UP ON ALL OF THIS TASTY GALENA.

WAIT, THIS IS GALENA?
ALSO KNOWN AS LEAD GLANCE OR LEAD SULFIDE. IT WOULDN'T NORMALLY BE DANGEROUS, UNLESS SOMEONE IS CHOMPING ON IT AND--

--FILLING THE CAVERN UP WITH LEAD DUST.
LEAD DUST CAN BE VERY DANGEROUS IF INHALED--
WAIT! THAT'S IT! WE'VE SOLVED IT!
JENN HAS LEAD POISONING! IT'S NOT EVEN A MAGICAL ILLNESS! I CAN CURE THAT!
THESE TURTLES EAT FAST. IF THERE WAS A BUNCH DOWN HERE, WE MIGHT HAVE BIGGER PROBLEMS.
UH, GUYS.
RUMMMMBLE
I THINK WE'VE GOT BIGGER PROBLEMS!
THAT... IS QUITE A LOT OF TURTLES.

WHOOOOAA!
AMBER! ARE YOU OKAY?
I'M FINE. ARE YOU OKAY?
THAT'S IT! THEY MIGHT NEED HELP. I'M GOING DOWN THERE!
NO, MOON, IT'S TOO DANGEROUS!

AND I CAN USE MY MAGIC TO HELP THEM! WHAT GOOD IS ALL THIS MAGIC IF I DON'T HELP OTHERS?
I'M GOING, TOO! I CAN'T LET OUR NEW FRIENDS BE HURT!

IF AMBIE IS GOING, THEN I'M GOING TOO!
PRINCESS FIONA FLOPPYEARS, YOU SIT AND STAY!

NOT THIS TIME, SISTER.
COME ON, INDY.

INDIANA EMBEREYES, I AM YOUR QUEEN!
IF YOU WANNA PROTECT US, YOU'LL HAVE TO COME TOO!

MY DEAR MAUD, WHY IS IT SHAKING LIKE THAT?
RUMMMMMBLE

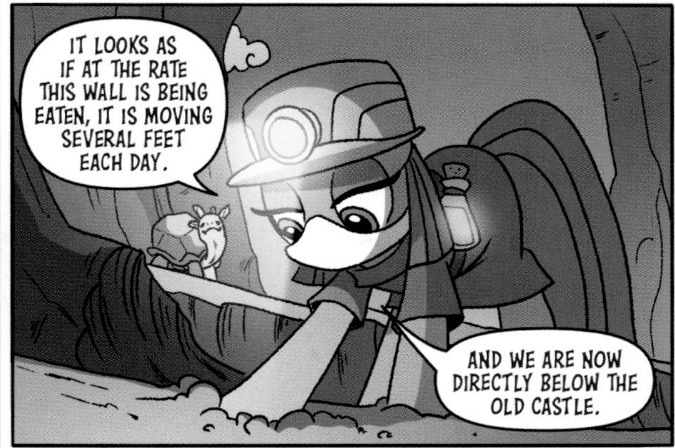
IT LOOKS AS IF AT THE RATE THIS WALL IS BEING EATEN, IT IS MOVING SEVERAL FEET EACH DAY.
AND WE ARE NOW DIRECTLY BELOW THE OLD CASTLE.

I BELIEVE THAT RUMBLE IS THE SOUND OF THE OLD CASTLE AND EVERYDOG IN IT PREPARING TO COLLAPSE INTO THIS PIT.
OH, IS THAT ALL? HOW ARE WE GOING TO STOP THAT?
CAN WE HELP?

WE HEARD WHAT YOU SAID.
I MAY NOT HAVE LIVED IN THAT CASTLE IN A WHILE, BUT I'M NOT ABOUT TO LET IT COLLAPSE!
I THINK I HAVE AN IDEA.

COME ON, WE NEED MORE ROCKS TO BRACE THE CASTLE!
YUP.
YOU GOT IT, SIS!
WE GOT IT, SIS!
RIGHT THERE, MOON. THAT'S PERFECT.
NOW, IF WE CAN JUST KEEP ANYTHING ELSE FROM GOING--
RUMMMMMBLE
OH, NO.
CRASH

IS EVERYPONY OKAY?
JUST A MOMENT, LET ME...

THERE WE GO. SISTERS, IS ANYCREATURE HURT?
WHERE ARE WE?

I HAVE THE BEST EYESIGHT, EVEN IN THE DARK. LET ME SEE...
WE'RE NEXT TO SOME SORT OF TREE. IT HAS SIX SPACES AROUND IT, AND OH!

OH NO, WHAT DID I DO? DID I BREAK IT?
LOOK, THIS PICTURE HAS FLOPPY EARS LIKE ME!

OH! I THINK I MIGHT KNOW WHAT THIS IS!
INDIANA, WOULD YOU COME OVER HERE QUICKLY?

MOON, YOU'RE CLEARLY MAGIC. AMBER WANTED TO TAKE CARE OF GUESTS, SHE'S KINDNESS. INDY CAN ALWAYS SEE THE TRUTH. FIONA TRIES TO MAKE EVERYDOG LAUGH AND BE HAPPY.
THOSE ALL LIT UP, AND BETWEEN THE TWO OF YOU, JENN WAS GENEROUS IN GIVING HER SISTERS WHAT THEY WANTED, AND KATHERINA WAS LOYAL IN TRYING TO PROTECT HER SISTERS.
BUT WHY AREN'T THEY LIGHTING UP? ARE THEY BROKEN?
NO, BUT PERHAPS I AM.
YOU ALL TOLD ME WHAT YOU NEEDED, BUT I THOUGHT I KNEW BETTER. MY LOYALTY TO TRADITION AND MY NEED TO PROTECT YOU ALL... IT KEPT ME FROM SEEING WHAT CAPABLE YOUNG DOGS YOU'VE BECOME.
I'VE SEEN IT VERY CLEARLY IN THIS CAVE.
AND JENN, MY STRONG, GENEROUS SISTER. YOU SAW WHAT I COULDN'T, AND IT MADE ME ANGRY AT YOU.
A TRULY LOYAL SISTER WOULD HAVE COME TO VISIT YOU, NO MATTER HOW ANGRY I WAS.
AND IF YOU HADN'T COME DOWN HERE, WE WOULDN'T HAVE KNOWN ABOUT THE TURTLES. OUR WHOLE KINGDOM WOULD HAVE COLLAPSED.
CAN YOU FORGIVE ME?

I WILL. I SHOULD HAVE A LONG TIME AGO.
YOU'RE NOT THE ONLY ONE WHO WAS WRONG HERE.
YOU WARNED ME IT MIGHT BE DANGEROUS, AND I DIDN'T LISTEN.
I CHARGED RIGHT IN WITHOUT PROTECTING MYSELF.
SOMETIMES BEING GENEROUS ISN'T JUST ABOUT GIVING TO OTHERS.
SOMETIMES IT'S ABOUT FORGIVING OTHERS, ESPECIALLY WHEN THEY CARE FOR YOU.
LET'S NEVER SHUT EACH OTHER OUT AGAIN.
AGREED.
BOOM
BOOM!
WHOOOOOOOOMMMMMM

THAT FEELS WAY BETTER.
SISTERS, LET'S GO SAVE THE CASTLE!

RUN! THE CASTLE IS COLLAPSING!
IT'S GONNA FALL ON US!
LOOK OUT!
GET TO SAFETY QUICKLY! MY SISTERS ARE TRYING TO SAVE THE CASTLE!
MAC, MEADOWBROOK, PLEASE HELP MY SUBJECTS!
COME ON, SISTERS! I BELIEVE IN YOU.

HERE, MY LIGHT IS WAY BRIGHTER NOW!
I CAN DIG SUPER-FAST!
CHECK OUT WHAT MY EARS CAN DO!
YOU THINK THAT'S COOL, CHECK OUT MY TAIL!
I WOULD LOOK, BUT MY EYES ARE PRETTY BUSY RIGHT NOW.

YOU'VE DONE IT! YOU'VE HELD UP THE ROOF! GOOD JOB, ROOF!
ROOF
ROOF
ROOF
ROOF
ROOF

I AM SO GLAD TO HAVE ALL OF MY SISTERS TOGETHER AGAIN.
ME, TOO.

BUT I'M NOT MOVING INTO THAT STUFFY, COLD CASTLE OF YOURS.
I WOULDN'T DREAM OF IT. ACTUALLY, I'M QUITE EXCITED ABOUT TRYING AMBROSIA'S SPA FOR MYSELF.

HOLD ON, IF WE'RE BACK TOGETHER, WHO'S GOING TO BE QUEEN NOW?
HMMM... WELL, I DON'T THINK HAVING TWO QUEENS SEEMS QUITE RIGHT. WHAT WOULD YOU THINK ABOUT...

...HAVING SIX QUEENS INSTEAD?

Dear Twilight,
Well, we've had quite the adventure here in Caninia.
We've literally bridged a gap between six sisters.

We're going to have to stay a bit longer because Meadowbrook is healing one of the princesses.
SAY, "WOOF."

Though hopefully not TOO much longer. I must admit that I find myself missing Sweetie Belle.
And I suspect Big Mac is missing Apple Bloom, but you'd hardly notice if you weren't paying close attention.
I MISS APPLE BLOOM!

Though, I am trying not to beat myself up too much about needing to stay.
Oh, and I nearly forgot.

We found something quite interesting here I can't wait to tell you about.
Ciao for now, Rarity
ANOTHER ONE!? THAT'S IT!
CALL A MEETING OF THE KNIGHTS OF HARMONY.
To be continued...

ABYSSINIANS

WHO WANTS CHOCOLATE WAFFLES?!
AS THE CAPTAIN OF THIS SHIP, I DEMAND WAFFLES!
AYE-AYE, CAP'N!
DASH INBOUND!
OH MY GOSH OH MY GOSH OH MY GOSH!
WA WA WA WA WAAAAA--
YOU GUYS! I JUST TALKED TO TWILIGHT, WHO HAS BEEN LOOKING INTO LEGENDS ABOUT TEMPLES LIKE THE ONE APPLEJACK FOUND IN--
UMMM... WHAT'S GOING ON?

OH, LOOK, EVERYPONY, RAINBOW DASH HAS MADE A DRAMATIC AND COMICAL ENTRANCE.
YOU KNOW WHO GENERALLY MAKES EXCELLENT DRAMATIC, COMICAL ENTRANCES?

THIS G--
NOW, DISCORD, YOU PROMISED NOT TO USE ANY CHAOS MAGIC WHILE WE WERE ON A MISSION TO A STRANGE COUNTRY.
THE ONLY TIME THEY'VE SEEN MAGIC WAS THE STORM KING AND... WELL... WE DON'T WANT TO REMIND THEM OF HIM, DO WE?

NOT IF YOU SAY WE DON'T, FLUTTERSHY.
ANYWAY, REMEMBER HOW ZECORA AND HER FRIENDS FOUND THAT TREE OF HARMONY, AND THEN--
I WONDER WHAT ZECORA'S FRIENDS ARE LIKE. I WANT TO MEET THEM! I HOPE THEY LIKE WAFFLES.

I HATE TO INTERRUPT, BUT WE BE APPROACHING THE DROP ZONE FOR TEAM FLUTTERSHY.
OOOH, IT'S ALMOST TIME TO GO TO ABYSSINIA!
CAPPER, YOU MUST BE SO EXCITED TO GO HOME!

YEAH... OF COURSE...
WHY ***WOULDN'T*** I BE?

CAPPER, MY FRIEND, THE GREAT AND POWERFUL TRIXIE HAS USED HER ASTUTE POWERS OF OBSERVATION ON YOU!
AND SHE HAS DIVINED THAT YOU ARE NOT ENTIRELY HAPPY ABOUT GOING BACK HOME.

DON'T WORRY ABOUT ME, TRIXIE. I'LL BE FINE.
INDEED. BUT AS SOMEPONY WITH A LONG LIST OF PLACES TO WHICH I AM NOT WELCOME TO RETURN, I KNOW THAT LOOK ON YOUR FACE.
AND AS A FRIEND, I WISH TO PROVIDE ASSISTANCE.

IT'S A LONG STORY, OH GREAT AND POWERFUL ONE--ARE YOU SURE YOU WANNA HEAR IT?
WE HAVE A LONG WALK, AND TRIXIE LOVES DRAMA. SPILL IT.

WELL, I NEVER REALLY HAD PARENTS. I RAN WITH A GANG OF STREET CATS IN PANTHERA, THE CITY WHERE WE'RE HEADED. WE STOLE TO GET BY.
THIS IS AN EXCELLENT SETUP. IF WE HAD BROUGHT POPCORN, TRIXIE WOULD BE CHOMPING IT.
WE MAY NOT HAVE HAD A HOME, BUT WE WERE FAMILY.

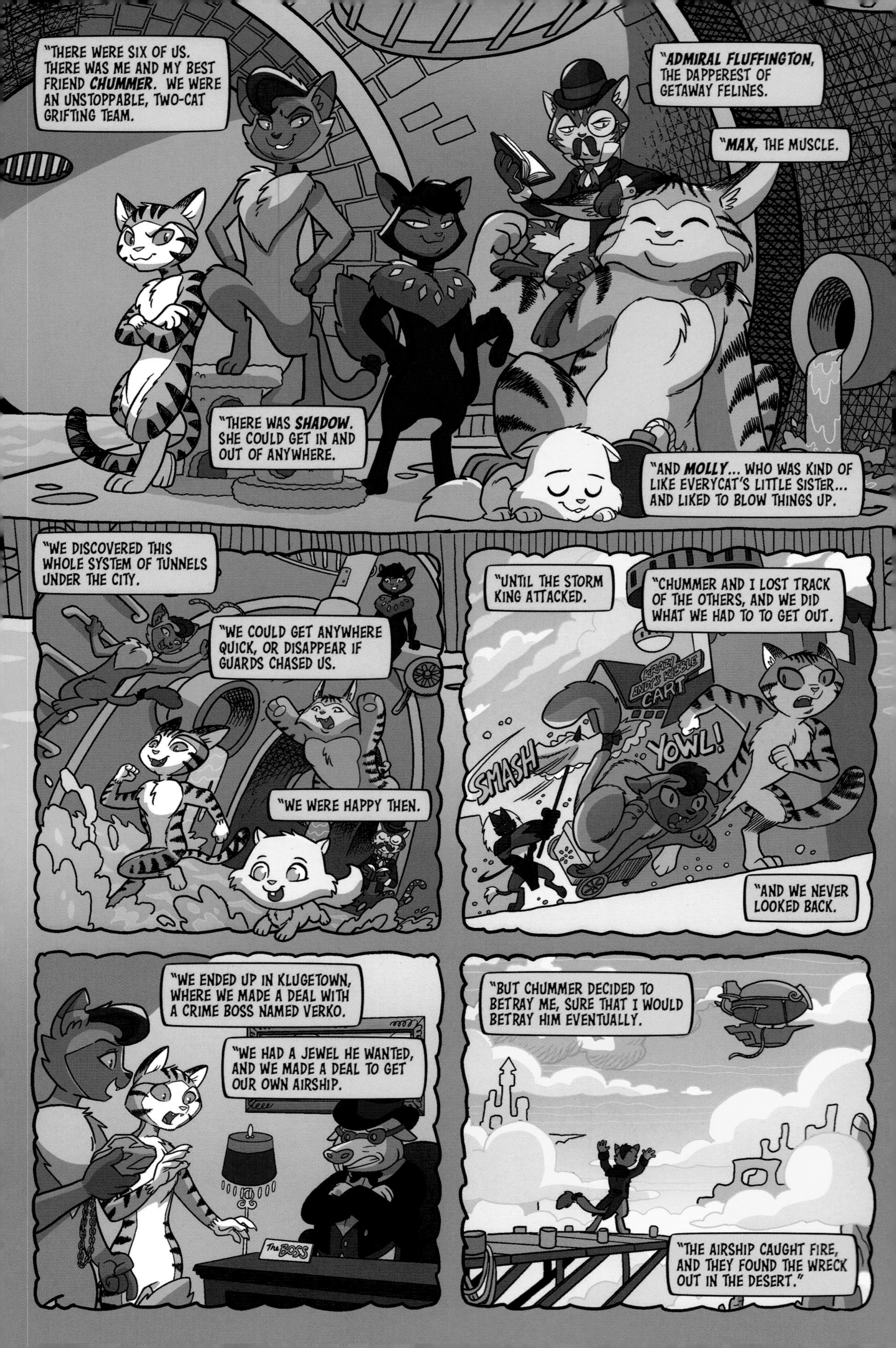
"THERE WERE SIX OF US. THERE WAS ME AND MY BEST FRIEND CHUMMER. WE WERE AN UNSTOPPABLE, TWO-CAT GRIFTING TEAM.
"ADMIRAL FLUFFINGTON, THE DAPPEREST OF GETAWAY FELINES.
"MAX, THE MUSCLE.
"THERE WAS SHADOW. SHE COULD GET IN AND OUT OF ANYWHERE.
"AND MOLLY... WHO WAS KIND OF LIKE EVERYCAT'S LITTLE SISTER... AND LIKED TO BLOW THINGS UP.
"WE DISCOVERED THIS WHOLE SYSTEM OF TUNNELS UNDER THE CITY.
"WE COULD GET ANYWHERE QUICK, OR DISAPPEAR IF GUARDS CHASED US.
"WE WERE HAPPY THEN.
"UNTIL THE STORM KING ATTACKED.
"CHUMMER AND I LOST TRACK OF THE OTHERS, AND WE DID WHAT WE HAD TO TO GET OUT.
KRAZY ANDY'S KIBBLE CART
SMASH
YOWL!
"AND WE NEVER LOOKED BACK.
"WE ENDED UP IN KLUGETOWN, WHERE WE MADE A DEAL WITH A CRIME BOSS NAMED VERKO.
"WE HAD A JEWEL HE WANTED, AND WE MADE A DEAL TO GET OUR OWN AIRSHIP.
The BOSS
"BUT CHUMMER DECIDED TO BETRAY ME, SURE THAT I WOULD BETRAY HIM EVENTUALLY.
"THE AIRSHIP CAUGHT FIRE, AND THEY FOUND THE WRECK OUT IN THE DESERT."

I DON'T KNOW WHAT HAPPENED TO THE REST OF MY FRIENDS. I ABANDONED THEM, JUST LIKE CHUMMER ABANDONED ME.
AND AFTER THAT... WELL... I DECIDED NOT TO HAVE FRIENDS. IT WAS EASIER THAT WAY.

AND SINCE THEN, IT WAS ONLY THE MAGNETIC MAJESTY OF TRIXIE THAT ALLOWED YOU TO BEFRIEND AGAIN?!
WELL, THERE WAS TWILIGHT AND HER FRIENDS, AND--

ATTENTION, MY ENTOURAGE!
HER ENTOURAGE?
ONCE WE ENTER AND ESTABLISH DIPLOMATIC TIES WITH THIS CITY, WE MUST FIND CAPPER'S FRIENDS AND REUNITE HIM WITH THEM, NO MATTER THE COST!

CAN WE TALK ABOUT THIS SOME FIRST? I'M NOT SURE IF THAT'S THE BEST IDEA.
WELL, YOU'D BETTER TALK FAST BUDDY, BECAUSE THIS MAP SAYS PANTHERA IS JUST OVER THIS HILL.
WHAT, REALLY?

I HAVEN'T SEEN IT IN YEARS. I WONDER WHAT IT WILL LOOK LIKE!
I'M GUESSING NOT AS COOL AS IT SOUNDS. PANTHERA SOUNDS VERY COOL. LIKE A PLACE WORTHY OF MY MAGICS.
REMEMBER WHAT WE TALKED ABOUT, DISCORD. CAPPER SAYS THERE'S NO MAGIC HERE, SO UNTIL WE HEAR DIFFERENT, NO CHAOS MAGIC.
OH, I'M SURE THEY'VE GOTTEN OVER THAT BY NOW.

OF COURSE, I HAVE BEEN KNOWN TO BE WRONG ON RARE OCCASIONS.
No Outsiders
or MAGIC ALLOWED
OH, NO.
CAT and FIDDLE

THINGS WERE BAD BEFORE I LEFT BUT...
THIS IS A HUNDRED TIMES WORSE. WE HAVE TO DO SOMETHING.
VIOLATORS WILL BE ARRESTED
OKAY, WE HAVE TO BE CAREFUL AND QUIET. WE'RE ALL GOING TO STAY TOGETHER UNTIL WE FIGURE OUT WHAT TO DO.
AND MOST IMPORTANT, DON'T DO ANYTHING SUSPICIOUS. WE DON'T WANT TO ATTRACT ATTENTION TO--
HEY! YOU LOT!

IS THIS SUPPOSED TO BE SOME KIND OF JOKE? ARE YOU JUST TRYING TO GET ARRESTED?!
OH, HELLO, OFFICERS. I DON'T KNOW WHAT YOU MEAN. I WAS JUST STOPPING TO TELL MY FRIENDS TO OBEY ALL OF THE RULES IN THE CITY.

I ALWAYS COMPLY WITH REGIONAL LAWS. SEE, WE'RE NEW IN TOWN, AND--
NEW IN TOWN? SO YOU LOT ARE OUTSIDERS! WE DON'T LIKE OUTSIDERS!
I UNDERSTAND. IF WE BROKE YOUR LAWS, I WOULD EXPECT YOU TO ARREST US!

SO, YOU'RE SAYING IF WE CAUGHT YOU BREAKING EVEN ONE LAW, WE WOULD BE JUSTIFIED IN ARRESTING YOU, AND YOU WOULDN'T RESIST ARREST.
YES, SIR. THAT'S EXACTLY WHAT I'M SAYING.
OKAY, THEN!

DO YOU KNOW WHAT LOITERING IS, OUTSIDER?
NO LOITERING! VIOLATORS WILL BE ARRESTED
OOOH! I DO! I DO!
THAT'S MAUD'S FAVORITE SPORT!

JUST GIVE THE WORD, FLUTTERSHY! THEY'LL BE COUGHING UP FURBALLS UNTIL HEARTH'S WARMING.
NO, DISCORD, NO MAGIC!
IF WE JUST GO QUIETLY, THEY'LL TAKE US TO THE CAT IN CHARGE, AND WE CAN--
NEVER!

THE GREAT AND POWERFUL TRIXIE DOES NOTHING QUIETLY!
THE GREAT AND POWERFUL TRIXIE WILL NOT BOW TO TYRANTS!
SHE'S USING MAGIC! WE NEED REINFORCEMENTS!

OH, TRIXIE.
SEE, IT'S FUNNY BECAUSE THE SECOND TIME WE MET TRIXIE, SHE TRAPPED US ALL UNDER A DOME AND--

MY MAGIC!
AS LONG AS YOU HAVE THIS COLLAR ON, IT WILL KEEP YOU FROM DOING MAGIC!

WAIT, WHAT?
WHY?!
SNAP SNAP SNAP

BECAUSE WE NEVER HAD MAGIC WITHIN OUR KINGDOM!
AND THE MOMENT MY PARENTS ALLOWED A MAGICAL CREATURE IN, THEY STOLE EVERYTHING!

CENTURIES OF GLORIOUS CAT RULE! KIBBLE IN EVERY POT AND CATNIP AS FAR AS THE EYE COULD SEE. WE HAD ALL OF THESE THINGS.
THEN MAGIC CAME AND DESTROYED IT ALL!

SO NOW, I HAVE BANNED MAGIC. MY GUARDS KEEP WATCH FROM THE GROUND AND THE SKY TO MAKE SURE THAT MAGIC DOES NOT RETURN.
NOKITTY WANTS TO RETURN TO THE DAYS OF THE STORM KING'S RULE, AND AS LONG AS KING MEOWMEOW IS IN CHARGE, THEY WILL NOT! SO, WE MUST BE VIGILANT!

NOW, WHO ARE YOU, AND WHY HAVE YOU BROUGHT THESE OUTSIDERS TO OUR HOME?
TELL ME, WHAT IS THEIR PLAN TO TAKE MY THRONE?

YOUR MAJESTY, MY NAME IS CAPPER, AND I WAS ONCE A LOYAL CITIZEN OF ABYSSINIA.
WHEN THE STORM KING CAME, MY FRIEND AND I RAN FOR OUR LIVES, AND ENDED UP ABOARD ONE OF HIS AIRSHIPS, WHICH CARRIED US FAR FROM HERE.

"I WENT THROUGH MANY HARDSHIPS, BUT EVENTUALLY MET TWILIGHT SPARKLE, THE LEADER OF THESE PONYFOLK.
"AND THOUGH SHE WAS IN DANGER, SHE WAS KIND TO ME AND... WELL, I BETRAYED HER.

"BUT TWILIGHT AND HER FRIENDS FORGAVE ME. THEY GAVE ME A SECOND CHANCE.
"THEY SHOWED ME THE VALUE OF FRIENDSHIP, AND LOYALTY, AND CARING.

"AND TOGETHER, WE UNITED AGAINST THE STORM KING AND BROUGHT HIM DOWN.
"YOU SEE, MAGIC MAY HAVE TAKEN THIS KINGDOM FROM YOUR PARENTS, BUT FRIENDSHIP SAVED IT."

THEY SHOWED ME THAT THERE WAS NOTHING GREATER THAN FRIENDSHIP. THEY SHOWED ME THAT THE CONNECTION BETWEEN CREATURES, CAT OR PONY OR... WHATEVER DISCORD IS... COULD BE UNBREAKABLE.
THEY SHOWED ME THAT FRIENDSHIP **WAS** MAGIC.

AND, YOUR MAJESTY, IF YOU ARE OUTLAWING MAGIC HERE, THEN YOU ARE OUTLAWING FRIENDSHIP!
SEE, YOUR PARENTS MAY HAVE NOT KEPT THE ENTIRE KINGDOM SECURE, BUT THEIR SUBJECTS LIVED IN HARMONY.
AND THAT WAS BECAUSE THEY WERE FREE TO LIVE AND CARE FOR EACH OTHER.

YOU SEE, I HAVEN'T BEEN BACK LONG, BUT I CAN TELL YOU THIS. THE STORM KING MAY BE GONE, BUT THESE CATS AREN'T FREE.
I'VE SEEN THE STREETS. I'VE SEEN THAT YOUR CATS LIVE IN FEAR UNDER THE CONSTANT, WATCHFUL EYE OF POLICE.

THESE PEOPLE MAY BE SAFE, BUT THEY'RE NOT HAPPY.
THE ONLY WAY FOR THIS COUNTRY TO BE AS GREAT AS IT ONCE WAS IS TO ALLOW THE RETURN OF MAGIC.

YOU MUST EMBRACE THE MAGIC OF FRIENDSHIP FOR THE GOOD OF ALL CATKIND.
WHAT DO YOU SAY, KINGY OL' PAL?

SLAM!
HUH.
THOSE SPEECHES ALWAYS WORK WHEN TWILIGHT DOES THEM.

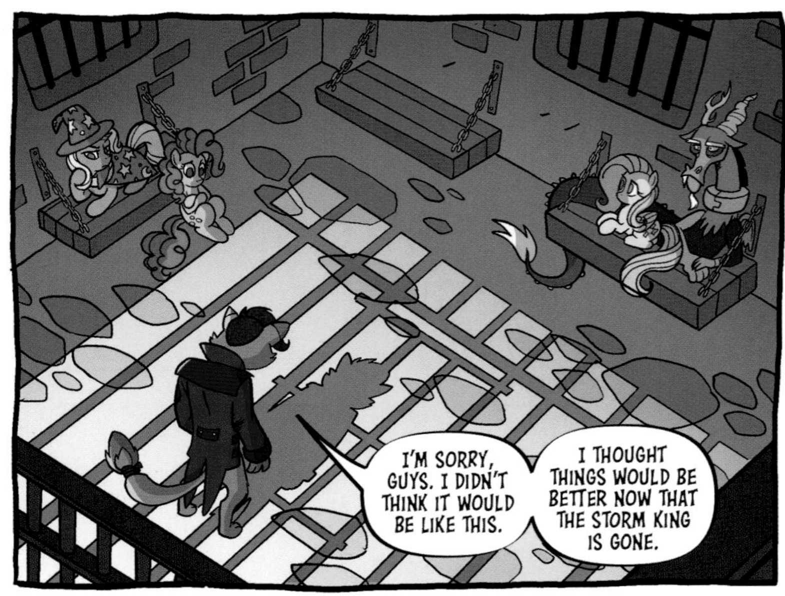
I'M SORRY, GUYS. I DIDN'T THINK IT WOULD BE LIKE THIS.
I THOUGHT THINGS WOULD BE BETTER NOW THAT THE STORM KING IS GONE.

IT'S NOT YOUR FAULT. YOU NEVER KNOW HOW OTHERS WILL REACT TO HARDSHIP.
RIGHT! LIKE THAT TIME TRIXIE TRAPPED US IN A DOME, AND SHE THOUGHT OUR SPIRITS WOULD BREAK, BUT INSTEAD WE WORKED TOGETHER TO...

DOES IT HURT?
IT'S JUST... STRANGE. IT'S LIKE I LOST MY ARM, EXCEPT...
I LOSE MY ARM ALL THE TIME FOR GAGS, AND I'VE NEVER LOST MY MAGIC BEFORE.

I'VE BEEN TRYING TO MAKE THIS WALL EXPLODE SINCE WE GOT HERE, AND IT HASN'T EVEN MOVED.
HONESTLY, THIS IS THE SINGLE WORST I'VE EVER FELT.

THE WORST YOU'VE EVER...
WHAT ABOUT WHEN YOU WERE A STATUE FOR A THOUSAND YEARS? OR THAT TIME YOU BETRAYED US AND--*WAIT.*
THIS ISN'T EVEN THE FIRST TIME YOU'VE LOST YOUR MAGIC! YOU'VE LOST IT *TWICE*!

WELL, SURE, IT SOUNDS BAD WHEN YOU SAY IT LIKE THAT.
BUT HONESTLY, EVERY OTHER TIME WAS BECAUSE OF MY OWN ACTIONS AND MISTAKES. I'M USED TO ACTING IMPULSIVELY AND BEING PUNISHED.

THIS TIME IT WAS BECAUSE I DIDN'T DO ANYTHING. YOU SAID, "DON'T DO MAGIC," AND I LISTENED.
NOW I'M IN JAIL.
I'M SORRY, DISCORD. I THOUGHT WE'D BE ABLE TO REASON WITH THEM. I THOUGHT WE COULD MAKE THIS BETTER.

OH, I'M NOT UPSET. THAT'S ACTUALLY WHAT'S SO STRANGE.
I DID SOMETHING STUPID *BECAUSE* I CARED ABOUT SOMEPONY, AND NOT JUST BECAUSE I WANTED TO.
THAT'S A NEW ONE FOR ME.

YOU KNOW, DISCORD, SOMETIMES YOU'RE SWEET.
I KNOW. I'VE BEEN TRYING TO MAKE UP FOR IT BY BLOWING UP THIS WALL, BUT--

BOOM!

DISCORD... DID YOU...?
IT DIDN'T FEEL LIKE IT WORKED, BUT I CAN'T ARGUE WITH THE RESULTS. MAYBE I OVER--

OH MY GOODNESS!
AH, SO SOMEPONY ELSE BLEW UP THE WALL.
WELL, IT HAD TO HAPPEN EVENTUALLY.

CAPPER, LOOK OUT!
AH!

CAPPER DAPPERPAWS?
UM... YES?

I CAN'T BELIEVE IT!
IT'S TRYING TO EAT HIM! HELP ME, PINKIE!
WAIT, WAIT, WAIT! I THINK IT'S A HUG.
THEY SAID IT WAS YOU, BUT I DIDN'T BELIEVE IT.
OF COURSE IT IS, YOU OLD STRAY!
SHADOW? SHADOW, IS THAT YOU?

GUYS, THIS IS MY OLD FRIEND SHADOW. SHE USED TO BE THE SMOOTHEST PICKPOCKET IN ALL OF ABYSSINIA.
WHAT DO YOU MEAN "USED TO BE"? I'M STEALING YOU ALL RIGHT NOW.
WHICH REMINDS ME!

WE GOTTA GET GOING BEFORE EVERY GUARD IN PANTHERA IS ON OUR BACK!
EVERYKITTY IS WAITING ON US!

WELL, FEARLESS LEADER?
OH GOODNESS... ON ONE HOOF, IT'S A JAILBREAKM AND WE'LL BE FUGITIVES.
BUT ON THE OTHER HOOF...

FOLLOW THAT CAT!
WEEE! IT'S A *GETAWAY!*

WEEEEE-OOOOOO!
OH NO, LIGHTS AND SIRENS!
NOW IT'S A PARTY!

HOW ARE WE GOING TO GET OUT OF HERE?!
KEEP EVERYCREATURE TOGETHER, AND DO WHAT I SAY, NO MATTER WHAT!

GUARDS!
GET DOWN!

OOOOOOH!

YARN?
IT'S A DISTRACTION!

COURTESY OF OUR DEAR **ADMIRAL FLUFFINGTON AND MAX.**

THERE'S STILL A FEW LEFT!
DON'T WORRY ABOUT THEM

I NEED EVERYCREATURE TO KEEP RUNNING, BUT CLOSE YOUR EYES.
OOOH! IS IT A SURPRISE?!
SORT OF. MOSTLY I DON'T WANT YOU TO GET BLINDED.

WE'RE ALMOST THERE!

JUST KEEP 'EM CLOSED AND LISTEN FOR THE EXPLOSION.

DON'T GO THROUGH THE WALL! OPEN YOUR EYES AND TURN RIGHT, NOW!
QUICK, DOWN HERE!

MOLLY! I CAN'T BELIEVE IT! LOOK HOW YOU'VE GROWN.
HEY, CAP! GOOD TO SEE YOU!
GUYS, THIS IS MOLLY, AND THE CATS IN THE AIRSHIP WERE ADMIRAL FLUFFINGTON AND MAX.
THIS IS MY OLD GANG!
OLD GANG, THESE ARE MY FRIENDS--TRIXIE, PINKIE, FLUTTERSHY, AND DISCORD.
THOSE EXPLOSIONS WERE AMAZING! WAS THAT YOU?
YEP, ALL TRICKS OF MY DEVISIN'. JUST LIKE THE LASER POINTER.
WE'RE GONNA BE SUCH GOOD FRIENDS!
THE GREAT AND POWERFUL TRIXIE APPLAUDS YOUR EXCELLENT DISAPPEARING ACT.
THAT MUST HAVE TAKEN SOME TIME TO PLAN.
WELL, I CAN'T TAKE CREDIT FOR THE PLAN. I'M MORE OF A FLY BY THE SCRUFF OF MY NECK TYPE.
IF IT WASN'T YOU, THEN WHO PLANNED IT?
THAT WOULD BE ME, OLD FRIEND.

IT'S GOOD TO SEE YOU AGAIN.
CHUMMER?
To be continued...

WELCOME TO THE ABYSSINIAN UNDERGROUND.

WOW, WHO ARE ALL THESE KITTENS?
KITTENS!
KING CAT HAS BEEN CLEARING THE STREETS, IMPRISONING EVERY STREET CAT AND KITTEN WITHOUT A HOME AND PUTTING A COLLAR ON EVERYTHING MAGICAL.

SPEAKING OF, LET THE CUNNING AND BRILLIANT ADMIRAL FLUFFINGTON GET THAT COLLAR OFF YOU.
THE GREAT AND POWERFUL TRIXIE LIKES YOUR STYLE, NEW FRIEND.

SO, ALL OF THESE KITTENS WERE RESCUED FROM PRISON, TOO?
MEH, SOME OF 'EM. WE TRY TO GET TO AS MANY AS WE CAN BEFORE THE KING DOES.
RAIDS LIKE THE ONE TONIGHT ARE RISKY, BUT WHEN WE HEARD ABOUT CAPPER'S SPEECH, WE KNEW WE HAD TO TRY IT.

AND THERE WE GO.
THANK GOODNESS!
EXCUSE ME, I DON'T SUPPOSE YOU COULD--

ALLOW TRIXIE TO--
TRIXIE, I--
--DEMONSTRATE HER MAGNIFICENT MAGICS--
THAT DOESN'T LOOK GOOD.
--BY HELPING YOU TO--

UH-OH.
OOOH, THERE'S NO WAY I CAN PICK THAT NOW.
WELL, FIGURE SOMETHING OUT! I NEED THIS OFF RIGHT NOW! I CAN'T TAKE IT ANYMORE!
I COULD MAYBE BLOW IT UP?
YOU'D PROBABLY TAKE HIS HEAD WITH IT.
THAT IS A RISK.
IT'S WORTH IT! I'LL JUST REATTACH IT AFTER--BUT I WON'T HAVE MY MAGIC UNTIL AFTER, SO MAYBE I WON'T-- WAIT!
WILL I NEVER HAVE MAGIC AGAIN?!
THIS IS YOUR FAULT, TRIXIE! I'M GOING TO--
STAY BACK!
DISCORD! WHAT'S GOING ON OVER HERE!
I WAS FINALLY GOING TO GET THIS COLLAR OFF AND GET REAL MAGIC BACK, BUT THIS SECOND-RATE SHOWPONY DECIDED TO STEP IN!
I AM NOT SECOND-RATE, AND I WAS ONLY TRYING TO HELP!

THAT'S ENOUGH!
DISCORD, WE WILL GET YOUR COLLAR OFF, I PROMISE. BUT FIRST, WE ARE REPRESENTATIVES OF EQUESTRIA, AND WE'RE SUPPOSED TO BE HELPING!
I UNDERSTAND YOU'RE BOTH UPSET, BUT I'VE BEEN UNCOMFORTABLE ON EVERY ADVENTURE I'VE EVER BEEN ON! WE NEED TO WORK TOGETHER!

NOW, MR. CHUMMER HERE HAS SOME INFORMATION HE'D LIKE TO SHARE ON HOW WE CAN HELP. I'D LIKE YOU ALL TO LISTEN.
RIGHT, WELL, THERE'S NO FORCE IN ABYSSINIA POWERFUL ENOUGH TO TAKE ON THE GUARD IN A FAIR FIGHT, AND THERE'S NO MAGIC.
EXCEPT, WE'VE BEEN DOING SOME RESEARCH, AND MAYBE THERE *IS.*

"WHEN WE WERE ALL KITTENS, THE GROUP OF US DECIDED TO MAP OUT THESE TUNNELS AS AN ADVENTURE.
"IN ONE OF THE TUNNELS, WE FOUND A STRANGE DOOR WITH NO WAY TO OPEN IT. WE DIDN'T KNOW WHAT IT WAS, SO WE LEFT IT ALONE.

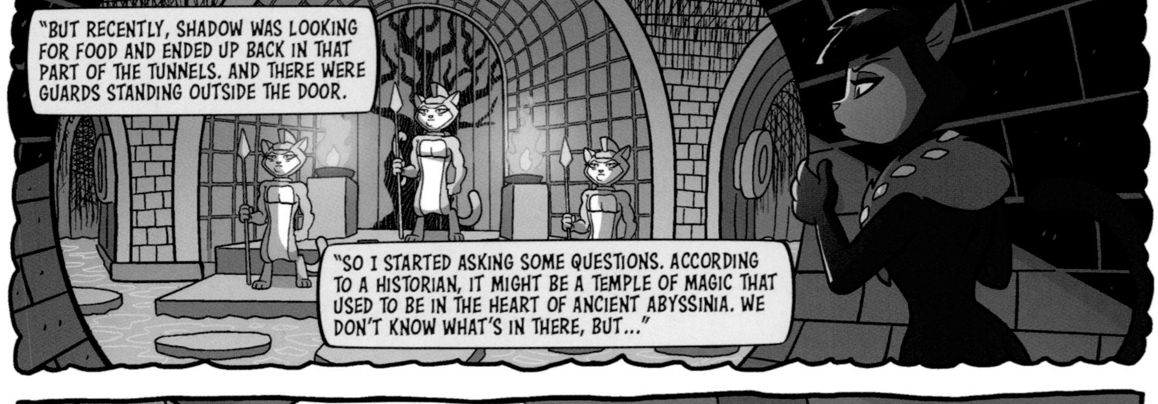
"BUT RECENTLY, SHADOW WAS LOOKING FOR FOOD AND ENDED UP BACK IN THAT PART OF THE TUNNELS. AND THERE WERE GUARDS STANDING OUTSIDE THE DOOR.
"SO I STARTED ASKING SOME QUESTIONS. ACCORDING TO A HISTORIAN, IT MIGHT BE A TEMPLE OF MAGIC THAT USED TO BE IN THE HEART OF ANCIENT ABYSSINIA. WE DON'T KNOW WHAT'S IN THERE, BUT..."

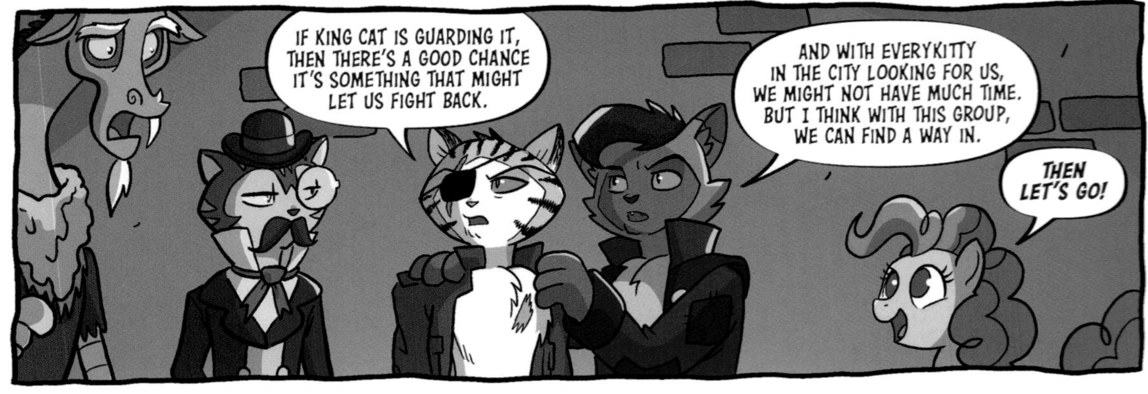
IF KING CAT IS GUARDING IT, THEN THERE'S A GOOD CHANCE IT'S SOMETHING THAT MIGHT LET US FIGHT BACK.
AND WITH EVERYKITTY IN THE CITY LOOKING FOR US, WE MIGHT NOT HAVE MUCH TIME. BUT I THINK WITH THIS GROUP, WE CAN FIND A WAY IN.
THEN LET'S GO!

WEE! I CAN'T WAIT TO SEE THE MAGIC TEMPLE!
ME NEITHER!
I KNOW YOU'RE A SORRY EXCUSE FOR A WIZARD, BUT I WANT YOU TO APOLOGIZE!
I TOLD YOU I WAS SORRY!
COME ON, SPORT, NO NEED FOR--
CHUMMER, I THOUGHT YOU WERE DEAD. HOW DID--
THAT'S IT!

I'M TAKING FLUTTERSHY HERE AND SCOUTING AHEAD! THE REST OF YOU STAY PUT!
WHY ME?
BECAUSE YOU'RE THE ONLY ONE THAT CAN BE QUIET.

SURELY, I CAN COME WITH YOU. I'M GREAT AT STEALTH.
WELL, YOU DON'T HAVE YOUR MAGIC FOR TELEPORTING, AND HONESTLY--
YOU'RE THE LOUDEST ONE. WE'RE GOING NOW.

WHILE WE WAIT, I WANT TO COME CLEAN WITH YOU, OLD FRIEND.
I'M SORRY FOR WHAT I DID TO YOU.

"WE'D LOST EVERYTHING. BEEN BETRAYED OVER AND OVER. I LOST MY FAITH IN FRIENDSHIP.
"I THOUGHT YOU'D TURN ON ME EVENTUALLY TOO, SO I HAD TO TURN ON YOU FIRST. THAT WAS THE ONLY WAY I THOUGHT I'D SURVIVE."

"I LEAPT FROM THE SHIP BEFORE IT CRASHED, BUT I HURT MY LEG AND COULDN'T WALK.
"I THOUGHT THAT WAS THE END FOR ME. BUT I WAS FOUND.
"THEIR NAMES WERE PEPPER AND SALTY. THEY CARRIED ME OUT OF THAT DESERT AND GAVE ME A PLACE TO RECOVER.
"PEPPER EVEN FED ME WHEN I COULDN'T WALK. SHE WAS THE KINDEST AND MOST FRIENDLY DOG I'VE EVER MET."

YOU GOT RESCUED BY ***DOGS!***
I WAS AS SURPRISED AS YOU. BUT THAT'S WHEN I REALIZED...

"NOT EVERYCREATURE DOES EVERYTHING FOR THEIR OWN BENEFIT. YOU CAN ***CHOOSE*** TO BE GOOD. YOU CAN CHOOSE TO BE A FRIEND.
"I LEFT PEPPER AND SALTY BECAUSE I KNEW I HAD TO TRY AND FIX EVERYTHING I'D MESSED UP."

I CAME LOOKING FOR YOU HERE, BUT WHAT I FOUND WAS OUR OLD FRIENDS AND A CITY IN NEED.
SO, I ASKED MYSELF, "WHAT WOULD MY BEST FRIEND CAPPER DO?" AND THE UNDERGROUND IS THE ANSWER TO THAT.
HEH. WHAT I REALLY DID WAS STAY IN KLUGETOWN AND CHEAT AND SCAM EVERYONE UNTIL THE PONIES CAME AND--
ARE YOU TWO STILL TALKING?

WE MADE IT ALL THE WAY THERE WITHOUT BEING SEEN OR HEARD. THIS PONY IS QUIETER THAN MOST CATS I KNOW.
I AM VERY STEALTHY.
BUT, THERE'S A PROBLEM.

"THEY MUST HAVE HALF THE GUARD DOWN THERE. I TOLD FLUTTERSHY IT WAS WAY TOO HOT. WE'D HAVE TO WAIT.
"BUT THEN SHE CAME UP WITH A PRETTY CLEVER PLAN."

OKAY, HERE IT IS.
FIRST THING'S FIRST--CAPPER, YOU NEED TO LEND DISCORD YOUR STYLISH JACKET.
MY JACKET? I DON'T GO ANYWHERE WITHOUT MY JACKET.

BECAUSE THE WHOLE THING RELIES ON DISCORD AND TRIXIE.
A VERY WISE DECISION.
THAT IS AN OBJECTIVELY TERRIBLE DECISION.

AND THESE TWO ARE GOING TO BE YOUR TEAMMATES.

YOU HEARD THE KING! NOW THAT THEY GOT THOSE OUTSIDERS, THEY'RE GONNA MAKE A PLAY FOR THIS PLACE. YOU HAVE TO--
GREETINGS, FURBALLS. IT IS I, THE GREAT AND POWERFUL--
DISCORD!
I HAVE COME TO CLAIM YOUR MAGIC FOR MYSELF AND LAY YOUR KINGDOM TO WASTE!
IT'S ONE OF THE MAGICAL OUTSIDERS! GET HIM!
WOW! MOLLY'S SMOKE BOMBS WORKED TO FOOL THEM--IT'S ALMOST OUR TURN!
IT'S TIME!
BUT HE STOLE MY ENTRANCE LINE! THEY'LL THINK I'M COPYING HIM!
ATTENTION MORTALS! YOU FACE THE MISTRESS OF CHAOS!
TRICK-SEE!
GET HER, TOO!

THEY THINK THEY CAN OVERPOWER US WITH TWO MAGIC USERS, EH?
THEY DON'T KNOW THE POWER OF THE--

ALL CLEAR!
WUMP

MY DISTRACTION IDEA WORKED!
LET'S HOPE WE CAN GET IN HERE QUICK AND QUIET BEFORE THOSE GUARDS COME BACK.
LET ME AT THAT DOOR. I'VE NEVER FOUND ONE I COULDN'T OPEN.

THIS MIGHT BE THE MOST COMPLICATED LOCK I'VE EVER SEEN.
I SAID IT WAS THE MOST DIFFICULT ONE, FLUFFINGTON.
IF YOU CAN'T GET IT, MOLLY LEFT ME SOME EXPLOSIVES.

BUT THEY HAVEN'T INVENTED A LOCK THAT OL' CAPPER COULDN'T PICK.
THAT'S PRECISELY WHAT I WAS TOLD.

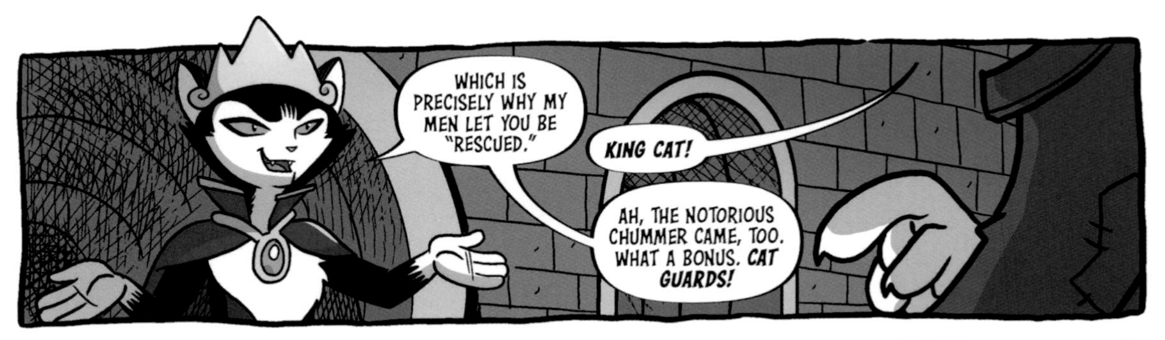
WHICH IS PRECISELY WHY MY MEN LET YOU BE "RESCUED."
KING CAT!
AH, THE NOTORIOUS CHUMMER CAME, TOO. WHAT A BONUS. CAT GUARDS!

I FOUND OUT ABOUT THIS OLD MAGICAL TEMPLE YEARS AGO. I'VE BEEN TRYING TO GET INTO THIS PLACE FOR AGES, BUT NONE OF MY GUARDS COULD PICK THE LOCK.
THEN, WHEN I FOUND OUT WHO HAD SCAMPERED RIGHT INTO THE MIDDLE OF MY KINGDOM, I MADE SURE WORD OF YOUR RETURN MADE IT TO YOUR OLD FRIENDS.

WELL, I'M DYING OF EXCITEMENT. LET'S SEE WHAT I CAME TO DESTROY.
BRING THEM IN, TOO. I WANT THEM TO WITNESS THE DESTRUCTION OF MAGIC IN THIS KINGDOM FOR GOOD.

OH NO!

SOME SORT OF MAGICAL TREE, HUH? I'LL HAVE TO GET RID OF THAT.
THAT'S A TREE OF HARMONY! IT'S A SOURCE OF MAGIC AND FRIENDSHIP! YOU CAN'T!
WATCH ME. BUT FIRST...
I HAVE TO LET EVERYCREATURE KNOW IT'S MINE.
SCRAAATCH
YOU CAN'T DO THAT!
OOF!
I AM THE KING, AND I WILL DO WHATEVER I WANT!
GET HER!
OH GOSH!
ALL RIGHT, FRIENDS, FLUTTERSHY IS ONE OF US.
IF THEY'RE GONNA GET HER, THEY'LL HAVE TO GET US ALL! WE WON'T LET KING CAT OPPRESS US ANYMORE!

TIME FOR SOME CHAOS!
WEEEE!
BUT YOU DON'T HAVE YOUR MAGIC!
IT DOESN'T MATTER! I'M GOING TO HELP FLUTTERSHY!
NO! NOT THE COLLAR AGAIN!
DON'T WORRY, TRIXIE! I'VE GOT 'EM RIGHT WHERE I WANT 'EM!
LET ME GO! I HAVE TO GET TO FLUTTERSHY!
HIT HIM WITH THE NIGHT STICK!

DISCORD, I DON'T THINK THINGS ARE GOING WELL. WE SHOULD HAVE HEARD SOMETHING BY NOW.
WAIT, I CAN FEEL IT-- FLUTTERSHY IS IN DANGER!
CAPPER, OLD FRIEND, I'M SORRY I PULLED YOU INTO THIS.
ARE YOU KIDDING? THIS IS THE ONLY WAY I'D WANT TO GO--FIGHTING FOR MY FRIENDS AND MY HOME.
STAY STILL!

CLANK!
CLANK?
WHAT KIND OF CREATURE HAS A NECK THAT GOES CLANK WHEN YOU HIT IT?
OH, I LOVE RIDDLES! I KNOW THE ANSWER TO THIS ONE--
--A FREE ONE.
BAD KITTIES.
SNAP
AH, THAT FEELS GOOD. IT'S JUST LIKE RIDING A HURRICANE.
WOW.

NOW WATCH AS I PUT AN END TO MAGIC IN THIS KINGDOM FOREVER!
WHAT IS THE MEANING OF THIS?
TAP
IT DOESN'T HAVE TO HAVE A MEANING.
IT'S CHAOS.
AND HE'S MY BEST FRIEND!

SOME BEST FRIEND. YOU KNOW, I USED TO HAVE ONE OF THOSE.
I'D LOVE TO HAVE ONE AGAIN, IF YOU CAN FORGIVE ME.

I THOUGHT I'D LOST YOU FOR GOOD, BUDDY.
I'VE DONE SOME PRETTY ROTTEN THINGS IN MY TIME, AND IF I CAN BE FORGIVEN, SO CAN YOU.
UH, GUYS...

THE FLOOR UNDER YOU IS GLOWING.
THERE'S SIX OF THEM! THEY MUST BE THE **ELEMENTS OF HARMONY.**

WELL, THAT ONE MUST BE CHUMMER'S BECAUSE IT'S STILL LIT UP.
HMMM... FROM THE POSITION, I THINK THAT'S LOYALTY.
OH, AND CAPPER, YOU FOUND YOURS!

HEH, HOW 'BOUT THAT. WHICH ONE IS THIS?
GENEROSITY. VERY FITTING, IF YOU ASK ME.

MOLLY IS LAUGHTER! I KNEW I LIKED YOU!

ADMIRAL FLUFFINGTON, YOU'RE KINDNESS.
WELL, NICE OF YOU TO SAY.

AND MAX, YOU'RE HONESTY!
HMMM... MAYBE THAT'S WHY I DON'T TALK MUCH.
THAT JUST LEAVES...

I DON'T UNDERSTAND. I DON'T KNOW MAGIC. I'VE NEVER DONE MAGIC. CATS DON'T DO MAGIC.
WHY ME?
BECAUSE FRIENDSHIP IS MAGIC...
...AND SO ARE YOU.
WHAT... WHAT'S HAPPENING?!
I KNOW WHAT WE HAVE TO DO. I CAN SEE IT IN MY MIND. CAN YOU ALL SEE IT TOO?
YES! I CAN! EVERYCAT, REACH OUT AND CONNECT TO YOUR ELEMENT. THE TREE WILL LIFT.
AND WHEN THE TREE LIFTS...
OH, THIS IS GONNA BE GOOD.
EVERYKITTY HOLD ON, THIS TEMPLE IS GOING UP.

RUMMMMBLLLLLLLE!

SCRRRRA
AAAAAAAPE!

SHHHHH
HHHHHUUUUUU!

MEOOOWWW! I FEEL LIKE I'M CHANGING!

WHAT HAPPENED TO ME?

HEY, DIDN'T YOU USED TO KNOW SOME CATS THAT LOOKED LIKE THAT?
AS A MATTER OF FACT, I DID. THEY DISAPPEARED, AND I NEVER KNEW WHAT HAPPENED.*
WELL, IT LOOKS LIKE THEIR MAGIC WAS SHUT AWAY.
*FOR MORE ON THIS, READ FIM#24.
YOU'RE SAYING... I CAN DO MAGIC?
WELL, IF I HAD TO GUESS, I'D SAY IT'S PROBABLY YOU AND A LOT MORE OF THE CATS OUT THERE.
AND NONE OF THEM KNOW WHAT JUST HAPPENED.

SEEMS TO ME LIKE THEY MIGHT NEED SOMEKITTY TO TELL THEM.
AND MAYBE THE WHOLE CITY CAN GET A FRESH START.

Dear Twilight,
Our adventure has reminded me of something very important.

It's that ALL friendships are magic.
Our friendship is great, and our story is important, but ours isn't the ONLY story.

Sometimes there are really important friendships that you think are lost forever--
--then they turn back up exactly when you need them.

And sometimes a friend can frustrate you, only to turn it around and come through in a pinch.
And you think--this is a friend who will go through anything for me. Maybe even my BEST friend.

And maybe this story is just a small part of a bigger story.
But it's hard to guess what could happen next.

And we should all be thankful for whatever time we have with our friends.
Your friend,
Fluttershy
CLICK
BOSS! WE GOT ANOTHER ONE!
To be continued...

COVER GALLERY

IDW

SEASON TEN
Episode 6

ISSUE
94
COVER A
$3.99

My Little Pony
Friendship is Magic

...O • BRECKEL

ART BY
TONI KUUSISTO

IDW

SEASON TEN
Episode 6

ISSUE
94
COVER B
$3.99

My Little Pony: Friendship is Magic

ZAHLER • KU

ART BY
BRIANNA GARCIA

IDW

SEASON TEN
Episode 6

ISSUE 94 COVER RI

my LITTLE PONY
Friendship is Magic

O · BRECKEL

ART BY
MUFFY LEVY

IDW

SEASON TEN
Episode 7

ISSUE
95
COVER A
$3.99

my LITTLE PONY
Friendship is Magic

ZAHLER • KU

ART BY
TONI KUUSISTO

IDW

SEASON TEN
Episode 7

ISSUE
95
COVER B
$3.99

My Little Pony
Friendship is Magic

10

O • BRECKEL

ART BY
BRIANNA GARCIA

IDW

SEASON TEN
Episode 7

ISSUE
95
COVER
RI

my LITTLE PONY
Friendship is Magic

ZAHLER • KU

ART BY
ERIN HUNTING

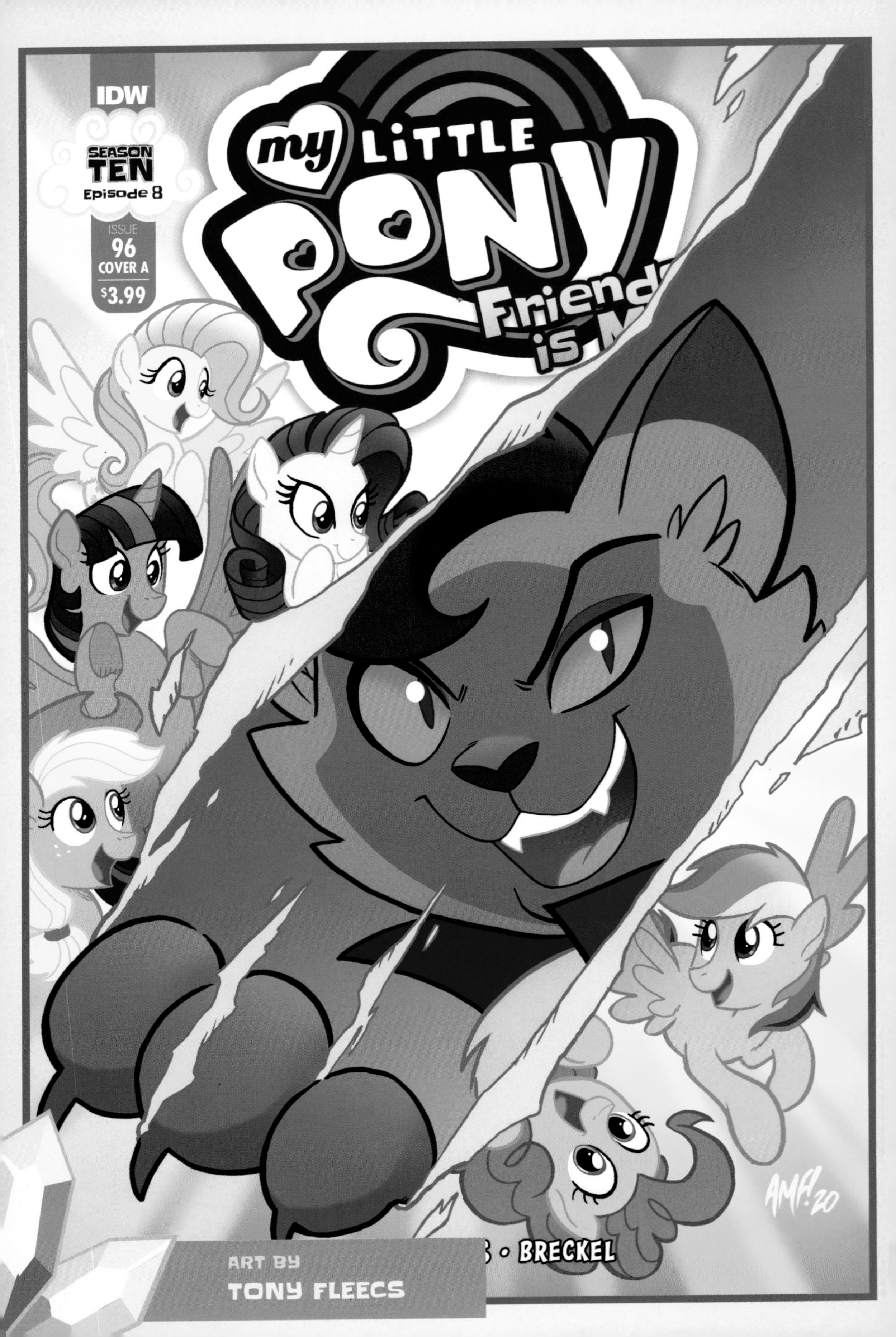
IDW
SEASON TEN
Episode 8
ISSUE
96
COVER A
$3.99
my LITTLE PONY
B • BRECKEL
ART BY
TONY FLEECS
AMF! 20

IDW

SEASON TEN
Episode 8

ISSUE
96
COVER B
$3.99

my LITTLE PONY
Friendship
is Mag

WHITLEY •

ART BY
JUSTASUTA

IDW
SEASON TEN
Episode 8
ISSUE
96
COVER
RI
my LITTLE PONY
Friendship is Magic
· BRECKEL
ART BY
MARY BELLAMY

IDW

SEASON TEN
Episode 9

ISSUE
97
COVER A
$3.99

my LITTLE PONY
Friendship

CATS 'R' MAGIC!

WHITLEY •

ART BY
TONY FLEECS

IDW

SEASON TEN
Episode 9

ISSUE
97
COVER B
$3.99

my LITTLE PONY
Friendship is Magic

· BRECKEL

ART BY
JUSTASUTA

IDW

SEASON TEN
Episode 9

ISSUE
97
COVER
RI

my LITTLE PONY Friendship is Magic

WHITLEY •

ART BY
MEGAN HUANG

IDW

2021

COVER A

$5.99

my LITTLE PONY Friendship is Magic Annual

BRECKEL

ART BY

BRIANNA GARCIA

IDW

2021

COVER B

$5.99

my LITTLE PONY

Friendship is Magic

Annual

WHITLEY •

ART BY

JUSTASUTA

IDW
2021
COVER RI

My Little Pony
Friendship is Magic
Annual

...I · BRECKEL

ART BY
TRISH FORSTNER

Friendship is Magic